His Last Drink

Also by Kim Antieau

Novels

The Blue Tail

Broken Moon

Butch

Church of the Old Mermaids

Coyote Cowgirl

Deathmark

The Desert Siren

The Fish Wife

The Gaia Websters

Her Frozen Wild

Jewelweed Station

The Jigsaw Woman

Killing Beauty

Mercy, Unbound

The Monster's Daughter

Queendom: Feast of the Saints

Ruby's Imagine

Swans in Winter

The Rift

Whackadoodle Times

Whackadoodle Times Two

Whackadoodle Times Three

Whackadoodle Times Galore

Nonfiction

Answering the Creative Call

Certified

Counting on Wildflowers

The Bird Hour

*Kim and Mario Build a Labyrinth and So Can You
(with Mario Milosevic)*

The Old Mermaids Book of Days and Nights

*The Old Mermaids Book of Days and Nights:
A Year and a Day Journal*

An Old Mermaid Journal

The Salmon Mysteries

Under the Tucson Moon

Short Story Collections

Entangled Realities (with Mario Milosevic)

The First Book of Old Mermaids Tales

The Second Book of Old Mermaids Tales

Tales Fabulous and Fairy

Trudging to Eden

KIM ANTIEAU

HIS LAST DRINK

Chapter One

"I had that dream again last night."

Jake's voice. Coming from the two sinks by the split bathroom in our bedroom. I cracked my eyelids open slightly. He was unseen behind the half-wall. Morning light slanted through the blinds, golden and filled with dust motes, turning the yellow walls of our bedroom nearly white. It was going to be another hot spring day in the Sonoran Desert.

I sat up in bed. It was so comfy here. No reason to be up this early. I wanted to go back to sleep.

Had Jake started talking to me before I was even awake? I didn't want to hear about another horrible nightmare, not first thing in the morning. I wanted him to be better, to be his old self. I wanted this part of our life to be over. It was exhausting.

My whole family was exhausting.

It was OK if Jake wanted to talk about it. Keeping it all inside wasn't good for him. The therapist and doctors said it wasn't good for any of us.

Sometimes I wondered if any of these so-called experts knew what they were talking about.

"I'm sorry you're still having those dreams," I said. "Did the gun go off this time?"

Jake stepped around the half-wall, a pair of scissors in his left hand. He was trimming his salt and pepper beard, as he did every morning. Every morning now that he was sober. Every morning now that he wasn't curled up into a ball somewhere fighting a panic attack. I squeezed my eyes shut for a moment. Didn't want to think about any of this the moment after I woke up.

"I grabbed the gun from Colin before it could go off again," Jake said.

Just as he had in real life.

"And it turned into a glass of beer."

Jake held the scissors a little higher as he stared out into space, remembering. It seemed like the blades caught the sun and gleamed back at me. Or maybe I was still half-asleep. Jake wore a fresh white T-shirt and a pair of black and white checkered boxer shorts. His thick black hair was slicked back away from his face. He was so beautiful: body and soul.

"Colin told me to drink the beer," Jake said. "I didn't want to, but Colin said, 'Go ahead. It can be your last drink.'"

"Little prick," I said.

"What?"

I shook my head. "Nothing. Go on. What happened next?"

"I drank it. And then I woke up."

Jake moved out of view again. I couldn't see his face, so I couldn't tell if the dream had bothered him. I started to say, "You might want to go to a meeting tonight." But I didn't. I crossed my middle fingers over my index fingers—the way I had when I was a kid and wanted to lie but didn't want it to count against me. Now it was a nervous twitch to keep myself from trying to control everything and everyone around me.

"That sounds like a better dream than the one where the gun goes off," I said.

"I guess," Jake said. "Although me taking a drink is almost as bad as the gun going off."

Our son Mattie walked into our room then. He was tall for being sixteen. He had dirty blond hair and bright blue eyes. Didn't look anything like Jake whose parents had come from Mexico many years ago. Or like me, really. My parents were short and Irish and French. Instead he looked like a model for some kind of Scandinavian sportswear company. None of us knew where Mattie got his height or his complexion. All through his years in school, coaches tried to talk him into playing sports. He wasn't interested. He wanted to be outside, mostly looking for birds, or inside reading, mostly about birds.

"Mom," Mattie said, looking down at his phone, "Jimmy says he heard an elegant trogon in Patagonia yesterday afternoon. Can I ditch school and go down there and search?"

I was up now and making the bed.

I heard water running. Then it was off. Jake came around the half wall, buttoning a rose-colored shirt he must have slipped on. He was wearing black jeans now. He grinned happily. Was he pretending for his son or was he really happy?

"I'm all for a skip day," Jake said. "Let's all go down. We can stop at Grandma and Grandpa's for lunch."

"I can't," I said. "I've got stuff to do."

"What stuff?" Mattie asked. "You don't have a job. You don't have any friends here."

The room got very quiet. We all stood there for a moment, not looking at one another.

Then I said, "I have friends. My darling teenage children are my best friends and would do anything for me." I grinned. Mattie looked sheepish.

Our daughter Jules came to the open door and leaned against

the door jamb, her arms folded across her chest. "You won't buy beer for us, so you can't be our best friend."

Jules was only a year older than her brother, but she had always seemed ancient. Ancient and bossy.

Mattie looked ready for school. Jules did not. Her clothes were slept-in wrinkled and mostly unbuttoned and her hair was uncombed. She took after me in that department. Neither of us much cared about our appearance as long as we were comfortable. She was tall, too, like Mattie, and athletic-looking, with thick brown hair and almost black eyes.

I picked up a pillow and threw it at her. She caught it and laughed.

"Of course I wouldn't buy you beer!" I said. "Why don't the three of you go to Patagonia? You can tell me all about it when you get back."

The kids didn't do much with their dad these days, so I tried—mostly unsuccessfully—to encourage them to be together as much as possible. I certainly didn't care if they skipped school.

I had wanted to homeschool them after everything happened, especially after we moved here. In fact, I hadn't wanted them to step into any school ever again. Not after Colin Moore walked into Jake's school, where Jake was principal in Portland, and first killed Mr. Miller, one of the maintenance men, and then raised up the gun to shoot Jake.

Only the gun had jammed. While Colin was looking down, trying to fix the weapon, Jake had grabbed the barrel and pulled the gun away from him. Colin reached into his backpack for another gun, but Jake and Mr. Bates, the science teacher, tackled him, and held him down until the police came.

Jake was hailed as a hero. He told me he didn't feel like a hero. Not then, not now. All these years later and he was still having nightmares. He kept hearing the click of the gun. Kept thinking he had been shot. Or the kids had been. Or me. He started to drink. Did drugs. Had a breakdown.

It was better now. He was better now. But nothing was the same. Nothing was ever good again. Not like it had been.

I sometimes wondered if it would have been better if the gun never jammed. Not because I wanted Jake dead. No! If the gun had gone off, if it had missed Jake, and he had still wrestled Colin to the ground, maybe things would have been different. Maybe better.

After. After it and after the worst of the pandemic, we moved from Oregon to Tucson to be closer to Jake's family. Jake worked in real estate now, and I took people on bird walks. Fortunately we had sold our home in Portland for a small fortune, and Jake had gotten a settlement from the school district. We were doing all right here, financially. For now. I didn't want to go back to my job as a public librarian, and I certainly didn't want Jake to work in a school again.

So we hung on day after day, trying to do normal.

Or we hung on one day at a time, as they say in AA.

The country falling into white supremacy and fascism was not helping us to do normal.

"It's still early," Jules said. "Let's go out for a bird hour before we go to school. I was outside, and Wizard said there's an indigo bunting out there somewhere."

"An indigo bunting?" Mattie said, suddenly excited. "Maybe we'll find a blue feather and life will be good again."

Jake winced.

"Not that life isn't good," Mattie said. "But remember what Grandpa says."

"'Find a blue feather and be happy forever,'" Jake said. "Particularly an indigo bunting feather."

"If only it were that simple," I murmured.

"Grandpa has many ideas on how to get rich and be happy,"

Jake said. "That's why he's digging holes everywhere he goes. I think the yard in our old house is all holes now. He dreamed once he would find buried treasure so he keeps looking."

I didn't know why Jake was telling us this. We had all heard his father's stories and reasoning about the holes.

"When I was a kid, he told me that story about indigo bunting feathers, and I looked for their feathers all the time. Never found any."

"You and I have looked for indigo bunting feathers many times at your parents' old house," I said. There were so many birds on their property. "We never found any."

"And we were happy anyway," Jake said.

"Yes, we were."

Yikes. I emphasized the word "were." Didn't mean to do that.

"Maybe we'll find that feather this morning, and all will be well," Jules said. "And remember, Wizard not only records the birds but everything you say."

"I'm gonna go look," Mattie said. He swiped his phone, turning on the Wizard birding app, no doubt, as he left our bedroom.

"Right behind you," Jake said. And then he was gone, too.

I looked at my daughter. We did not get along. I was constantly wondering what was up with her—today in particular. She suddenly wanted to go out birding? When the kids were little, we spent many hours combing the woods in Washington and Oregon or the desert when we visited Jake's family, looking for birds and other wildlife. Jules had left that all behind in her pre-teens. She often made fun of us now when we went birding.

"What a bunch of birdbrains," she'd say. Her teenage wit was not exactly stellar. "I've got better things to do."

Now I pulled a shirt from my closet and a pair of jeans from my dresser and quickly put them on.

"Why are you being so nice?" I asked. I grabbed my phone—for the Wizard app—and Jules and I walked down the hall, through the great room, and then out the back door.

"I'm nice," Jules said. "Dad seemed a little down last night. Thought he could use some family time, and Mattie doesn't like being alone with him."

"I've noticed that," I said. "Why?"

Jules shrugged. "He doesn't want to be responsible for him, I guess."

We stood under the overhang for a moment looking out. We lived on the east side of Tucson, in horse country even though we didn't board any horses. We had four acres filled with cacti, various types of mesquite, palo verde, and other trees and bushes. This meant we had lots of birds.

I glanced down at my phone. Wizard had picked up the song or call of an indigo bunting. I felt a hiccup of joy. The male indigo bunting especially was so gorgeous: bright blue.

"OK," Mattie shouted. He and Jake were about 50 feet ahead of Jules and me. "We start bird hour now. 6:05 a.m."

I waved to Mattie and Jake to let them know we heard. Bird hour meant we couldn't talk about anything but birds for an hour. We weren't even supposed to think about anything except birds for an hour. It was a way to help us all relax a bit and forget about the shooting, Jake's troubles, what was happening in our country, or anything else mundane and anxiety-inducing. We could forget about everything except the flying dinosaurs called birds.

Jules and I stepped off the porch and followed the narrow trail. I watched Jake and Mattie ahead of us. When had Mattie gotten so much taller than his father? Was Jake shrinking?

"The first time I saw an indigo bunting was with your father," I said to Jules.

Jake and I had met at University of Arizona 25 years earlier.

He was studying to be a teacher and me to be a librarian. We both wanted to be writers, but we figured we should have some skills that could get us actual jobs. After we had been dating for a while, he took me down to the small town of Patagonia near the Mexico/U.S. border to meet his parents, Santiago and Isabella Acosta.

"You've told me the story," Jules said. "Many times. You saw these beautiful blue birds eating at Grandma and Grandpa's feeder, and Dad told you that every blue bird in the world is a blue bird of happiness, especially an indigo bunting. You decided right then and there that Dad was your guy."

I laughed. "I guess I've told that story a lot."

She nodded. "And every time I hear it, I think you must love Dad a lot. Then I remember you cheated on him and nothing was ever the same."

In that moment, I wanted to slap her. I had never had that desire before, had never even spanked my kids, but now I was tempted.

I didn't slap her.

"First, that is not bird hour talk," I said. "Secondly, you have no idea what you're talking about, Juliet Marie. And I don't appreciate you bringing this subject up again and again."

Ahead of us, Mattie pointed and then Jake glanced back at us.

"There's two of them," Jake called. "The male is so blue!"

"Does Dad know Tom Kelly is here in Tucson?" Jules asked. "Does he know you've been seeing him?"

I stopped walking and looked at my daughter. "My private life is none of your concern. I have known Tom since I was a kid, younger than you are now. When he comes to town—whether it's here or when we lived in Portland—I see him. It's completely innocent and none of your business. Keep your hands and your nose out of my phone and my stuff."

How else could she have known that Tom Kelly was in town except by looking at my phone?

"I've got to go to practice," Jules said. "Tell Dad I'll see him later."

"Oh no," I said. "You started this bird hour. You are gonna finish it. Catch up with your brother and father and look at the fucking bird of happiness. Act happy about it. Do it for your dad."

Jules glared at me, but then she hurried away to be with her dad and brother.

I watched them for a few moments, a ball of anxiety forming in my stomach, and then I turned around and went back to the house.

Chapter Two

I supposed I should have known something bad was going to happen then, that morning. But Jules being bitchy to me was nothing new. Jake seemed his old self, almost. He drove the kids to school after the bird hour—no one found any bird feathers, blue or otherwise—and then he came home and made breakfast. We sat at the counter eating baked potatoes and scrambled eggs and talking about—about what? I don't remember. The weather? The kids? Birds?

We didn't talk about me being anxious. Because it wasn't new. Ever since the shooting, I felt like something bad was going to happen every minute. Maybe every other minute now. Before the shooting, I thought I was prepared. The world was a scary place. I wasn't one of those people who thought "it can't happen to me. To us." I knew it could happen. I knew bad could happen because I grew up with bad.

My own mother was ill most of her life. Or at least most of her life with me. It was almost like not having a mother. Even when she was physically present, it felt like she had left the building. She struggled. She tried to be in the world. I look back at times in my life when I knew my mother was there, and I can't see her in my mind's eye. That haunts me to this day: How often did I ignore her, not pay any attention to her, until she disappeared from the world, long before she actually died?

My mother was not like everyone else. She was shy but outspoken, too. She often asked questions of my friends that embarrassed me. She used our bedroom walls as her canvas.

Once she painted Olympia on our wall. Olympia was naked, just as Manet had painted her, with a string bow around her neck and a red flower in her ear.

When I had friends over, they looked at the painting and said, "My mother would wash my mouth out with soap if I painted that."

I said, "My mom is the one who painted this."

She seemed to fade after a time. She couldn't find a creative outlet in her role as mother and wife. She didn't have the education or the know-how to get a job. Not back then. Or maybe she was too exhausted by illness to do anything else.

The world had no use for her. She didn't fit in anywhere. When I was a kid, it irritated me that she wasn't like other mothers. Later I realized she wasn't a monotone person in a world that only wanted monotone, monochrome, monoculture. Her mental and physical illnesses melded into one big illness. They crushed all the color out of her until she became monochrome.

After a while, no one paid any attention to her. Even her own family. It was almost as though she didn't exist, had never existed. We were the only proof—her children—that she had ever been. Us and her art. She had painted over Olympia long before I left home. After she died, we found drawings she had made, photographs she had taken, letters she had written about her dreams. At first, it all reeked of loss and failure. Many years later when I looked at them again, I saw how much she had tried to find her way in the world despite everything.

The thing was the world didn't care how much we tried. Or how much we didn't try.

I remember once my mom and my dad visited me while I was going to school at the University of Arizona. She took me clothes shopping. I didn't care about clothes, and she didn't much either, but it was something we could do together.

As she picked out a blouse and a pair of pants for me, I asked her if she was happy. She held the clothes up to me and said, "I don't think about whether I'm happy or not." She said it so matter-of-factly, with no expression. Did that mean she was happy so she didn't think about it? Or did it mean she had been sick and miserable for so many years that she didn't think about it?

At the time, it was the saddest thing I had ever heard. And then, she seemed to disappear more and more after that. Now I didn't think about whether I was happy or not either. I thought about whether my family and I were safe or not.

Sometimes, Jake had that same expressionless look my mother had. Sometimes since the shooting when I looked in the mirror, I saw it on my own face, too. That lack of expression.

When our family didn't seem to get over it quickly enough, people started ignoring us. We were supposed to suck it up. To get on with it. To be heroes and the wife and children of a hero. To not be changed by the violence.

I wanted that. I wanted our life to go on as it had before. But I couldn't shake the fear. Jake couldn't shake the fear. Or the reality. He kept hearing the click of the gun. I kept hearing the click of the gun even though I hadn't been there. Even though I hadn't seen Mr. Miller die. Hadn't seen him fall to the hallway floor like a puppet whose strings had been cut. Hadn't seen his red plaid shirt darken as time went on.

His name was Horace Miller. All of us called him Mr. Miller.

He had been at the school forever. Our kids knew him even though they didn't go to Jake's school.

At Mr. Miller's wake, Jake told everyone about the time someone had sprayed "fuck you" on the outside north wall of the school in big bright orange letters. It was there for weeks. Jake kept bugging Mr. Miller to clean it up. It didn't happen and it didn't happen. Then one morning, the school started getting calls about the graffiti on the north wall.

"Horace," Jack said. "You gotta fix that."

"It's fixed," he said. "It's all better."

Mr. Miller led Jake out to the north wall. In bright orange letters were the words "book you."

"See, I closed up the letters. Now it's very educational."

Mr. Miller was very pleased with himself. Jake told him to clean off all the lettering. No one had called the school about "fuck you," but they got half a dozen calls about "book you."

At Mr. Miller's wake, Jake said he was sorry he had made him take it down.

Late one night after Mr. Miller died, Jake took a can of orange spray paint and wrote "book you" on the north wall.

That was when everyone decided Jake was crazy. And a drunk. They didn't want anything else to do with him. He was no longer a hero.

Sometimes even I wished he would get over it. Although I never said that to him.

I thought of Horace Miller every day. Probably Jake did, too. He didn't tell me much of what he thought about any more. Maybe he sensed I was tired of it all.

I remember now: At breakfast that morning after the bird hour, after he took the kids to school and we had breakfast together, I asked him his plans for the day.

"I'm showing a house in Vail," he said. "I shouldn't be long. We could meet for lunch back here."

I shook my head. "I'm having lunch with Tom Kelly. Remember?" I said it casually. It was nothing. Just lunch with an old friend.

"You're actually going to eat inside a restaurant?" Jake asked. "That's a big step." Since the pandemic, I didn't like being in crowded situations inside buildings.

"No," I said. "We'll eat outside somewhere. Probably Agua Caliente Park. I'll text him later."

Jake pushed away his plate. His meal was half-eaten.

"Does it bother you?" I asked. I put my hand over his. He winced slightly.

"It's not my favorite thing," he said, "but as long as you're not sleeping with him, I'm okay with it."

"You sound like Jules," I said. "Can you have a talk with her about this? She has implied several times that I cheated on you, and that's why you had your troubles."

Jake looked at me. He half-grinned. "My troubles? That sounds like I'm Ireland."

"I don't think Ireland has troubles anymore," I said. But we do I didn't say out loud.

"What do you want me to say to her?" Jake asked. "She knows the truth. She's razzing you. It's what teenagers do."

"I want you to tell her to quit being a bitch to her dear old mother," I said.

"You did sleep with Tom," Jake said. He got up, took his plate to the sink, and left it there. He didn't put his half-eaten food in the garbage which he usually did. Should I have realized then something else was going on?

I was too irritated to notice anything. I was not going to have another conversation about Tom with any member of my family.

"Jules has a baseball game tonight," I said. "Are you going?"

He nodded. "Of course. Do you want to meet there?"

I didn't want to go at all, but I said, "OK."

"I'm thinking of applying for a teaching job," he said.

"Where?"

"Here," he said. "They're short teachers. Since the pandemic."

"And since all of the school shootings," I said.

"We're gonna run out of money," Jake said. "It's not like these kids are going to get rich any time soon."

I almost laughed.

"You got that right," I said.

Jake smiled.

"I'm only thinking about it," he said.

"I thought we were going work at our writing careers," I said.

"What careers?" he asked.

"The ones that died when we had kids," I said.

"And then they turned into teenagers and that really killed the dreams dead."

Jake came around the counter and put his arm across my waist and kissed the top of my head.

"I've been writing a little," he said.

I looked up at him. "That's great. Can I read it?"

He kissed my mouth. "Sure. Soon. What about you? What creative things have you been up to?"

"Not saying irrevocable things to our daughter," I said. "That requires a lot of creativity and restraint on my part."

"I'll talk to her," Jake said. "But you having lunch with Tom isn't gonna help."

"It's none of her fucking business," I said. "Did you tell her that I was meeting Tom?"

"No, why would I tell her?"

"She found out somehow," I said. "So I'm guessing she snooped at the calendar on my phone."

Jake moved away from me. I sounded angrier than I meant

to. Truth was I could not stand being around my own daughter. She was rude. She was bratty. She was disrespectful. I wanted to shake her and say, "What have you done to my real daughter? Bring her back!"

I couldn't call my own mother and get advice. Since she was dead. I tried to remember what I had been like as a teenager, but I had little memory of how I treated my parents: except that I ignored my mother. I almost wished Jules would ignore me instead of picking at me. She didn't pick at her father, only me. Probably thought he was too fragile. I was the ironman of the family. I was the one who was supposed to do everything, figure it all out, make certain we were all left standing.

Except that was an impossible task when the world was tipped on its side. When it was impossible to know if someone had a gun. Or a disease. Or a prejudice they were ready to act on.

In any case, my daughter didn't like me. And nothing I did or didn't do was going to change that. I had to wait until she was old enough to understand life better or old enough not to have so many hormones coursing through her body.

"Mattie was right," I said. "I have no friends. I know no one. Tom is in town on business. I want to have a conversation with someone besides people in my family."

"You can go back to work," Jake said, clearly ignoring the part about Tom. "You'd see people all the time. I know the public library is looking for librarians."

"Are we having this conversation now?" I asked.

We both had worked in public service jobs since we were out of college. They paid crappy, but we thought we were making a difference—and we wanted to be home for the kids.

I shook my head. "You were almost killed. Remember the bullshit we both dealt with all the years before the shooting, too. Not only from the public but the people we worked with. So many dangerous people. So many assholes. No. I'm not putting myself out as a target again. And I don't want you to either."

I said it all in a rush. My heart was racing. I felt like I could hardly breathe.

"I can't even stand the kids going to school," I said. "Every day I wonder if they'll come home to us or not."

Jake rubbed my back gently. "We have got to get back to normal sometime."

"Normal? What is normal?" I asked. "The planet is burning. Some days we can't even go outside because of the smoke or the ozone pollution. We have mass shootings every other day, it seems. One pandemic after another keeps circling the globe. People are openly racist, homophobic, misogynist. Right-wingers have taken over the government. ICE is kidnapping people off the street. If this is fucking normal, I don't want it."

Jake looked surprised. I had kept these feelings to myself because I didn't want him to be triggered, didn't want him to feel like he had to fix it all.

"Sweetheart, we have to find normal for <u>us</u>," he said. "We have to have some joy."

"Having lunch with Tom Kelly will bring me joy."

Jake blinked quickly. As though he had been slapped.

"Not that you all don't bring me joy," I stuttered. "It's just that he's known me since I was a kid. I don't have to be anyone but myself around him."

Jake frowned. "Who do you have to be for us? For me?"

"Everything."

"And with Tom?"

"Nothing," I said. "I can be nothing."

I couldn't fail Tom. Because he expected nothing of me or from me. I was nothing to him. Sometimes I wanted to be nothing to someone.

Jake sighed. I hadn't meant to say any of it out loud. Jake did not need any more burdens.

"Don't pay any attention to me," I said. I pushed away from the counter, picked up my plate, and took it over to the sink. "I'm blowing off steam. Jules got under my skin. Is it too late to put her up for adoption?" I turned around and smiled. I hoped it looked like a real smile.

"Never too late," Jake said.

We walked toward each other and put our arms around the other.

"After the game, let's get a pizza and have a cozy night in front of the TV," Jake said.

"That'll be nice," I said. "Especially if Jules goes out with her friends afterward. Although I don't know how on Earth she has friends if she treats them the way she treats me."

Jake laughed. "I gotta go. Keep in touch."

"I'm not the one who constantly loses my phone," I said.

"I don't lose it," Jake said. "I don't remember it. When we were kids, we didn't carry around anything but our charming personalities."

"Maybe that's all you carried," I said. "I had my wallet and a switchblade."

"What? You never told me that. A country girl from the Midwest?"

"I lived an hour from Detroit," I said, "and besides, girls and women were getting killed all the time when I was growing up. I figured I wasn't gonna make it easy for anyone who came after me."

"Seriously. Did you know how to use a switchblade?"

"Sure," I said. "Well, I used to. It's been decades. I opened it accidentally in my pocket one day and decided to ditch it."

"You know I support you doing whatever you need to protect yourself and to feel safe."

"Even get a gun?"

"Even get a gun," he said.

I shrugged. "If I could mistakenly open a switchblade in my pocket, imagine the damage I could do with a gun."

"I don't need to imagine it," Jake said. "I've seen the damage a gun can do."

We looked at each other.

"The world sucks," I said.

Jake nodded. "A lot of it does."

"I want to live someplace where the patriarchy has fallen. Where women don't have to carry weapons to protect themselves. Where people love each other and are at peace."

"The problem is that you don't love people and you're not at peace," Jake said.

"That is not the problem," I said. "I don't love people because they're assholes, and they're out to get us. And I'm not at peace because people are assholes and they're out to get us."

"You know what you're feeling are classic signs of PTSD," Jake said.

"And also classic signs of someone who understands reality," I said.

I wasn't sure how this morning had gotten so off kilter— with me talking about how terrible the world was to my husband who was trying to stay sober and upbeat about life. I needed to get it back on track. I was saying how I felt, and I couldn't seem to stop.

They say the truth will set you free.

Maybe they should say the truth will set you free and then your world will fall apart. Again.

"I'll see you at the game," Jake said. "I'm meeting Stuart at Lucy's before the game. He wants to talk to me about something."

"Lucy's?" I said. "Isn't that a bar?"

"Stuart suggested it," Jake said. "He's the boss, so I agreed. No big deal. Don't worry. It'll be my last drink."

"Not funny," I said.

He grinned. "It's a little funny."

"Not even."

"Call me if you need me."

I didn't watch him leave. I never did. I had heard once that it was bad luck to watch a loved one go. So I never watched. Or seldom did. Same thing with the kids. Usually I called after Jake, "Come home to me," and he would say, "Always." But I didn't say it on this particular morning. Got distracted by the breakfast dishes. Or maybe it was a text. I dunno.

A little later, I remembered I had forgotten, so I whispered to myself, "Come home to me." I imagined Jake saying, "Always," but it was too late. He was already gone.

Chapter Three

I asked Tom to meet me in Agua Caliente Park which was a few minutes from our house. I didn't know much about the place except at one time it had had a hot spring and cold spring and someone had planted lots of palm trees. As I understood it, palm trees weren't native to Arizona except in some riparian areas. Still, some birds liked them—particularly great horned owls and hooded orioles—and they looked pretty in this park.

The whole park seemed out of place in Tucson, but then so did I. So I liked the park, this oasis snuggled up against the foothills of the Catalina Mountains.

I chose a picnic table far enough away from the water that we wouldn't be disturbed by people or their dogs but close enough to the trees to get shade.

Tom got there only a few minutes after I did. I waved. I liked that about him: He was on time. He hadn't ever kept me waiting. Neither had Jake, except when he started drinking. Then I never knew when or where he was.

Tom smiled and waved. He held up a bag of takeout in his

other hand. He looked like an old high school beau should look, at least for a woman my age. He had a bit of a paunch, and his brown hair was turning gray. He looked like he had played football in high school, and he had. Now it made his knees creak occasionally and ache most of the time.

He gave me a bear hug and kissed the top of my head. I held on to him a little too long maybe, but he didn't let go either. It felt good.

Then the hug was over. Tom dropped the bag onto the shaded table and looked around. At the palm trees. At the blue blue sky. At the mountains.

"Wow," Tom said. "I could get used to this. It's still below freezing in Michigan."

"You wanna walk around or eat?" I asked.

"Look at me," he said as he sat on the picnic table bench. "I want to eat."

I sat across from him as he opened the bag and began pulling out other bags.

"You said to get anything," he said. "So I brought tacos and burritos. Some are bean, some chicken. I got beef for me." He pulled out two cans and handed one to me. Cold beer. I opened the can and took a gulp. Tasted awful and delicious.

I unwrapped a taco. I stared at it for a moment, wondering if it was safe to eat, and then I closed my eyes and bit into it.

"You look good," Tom said. "Things getting easier?"

"Sure," I said. My eyes watered with tears. I quickly blinked them away. Tom reached across the table with his left hand and wrapped his thick fingers around the fingers of my right hand. We ate in silence for several minutes. I sighed and chewed and sighed and chewed.

"Good choice," I said. "You'll have to tell me where you got them."

He shrugged. "Some place on a corner somewhere near my hotel."

I laughed. He brought my hand up to his mouth and kissed my palm. Then he let go of it so he could eat his next burrito with both hands.

"Tell me everything," he said. "I want to know."

"Give me a break," I said. "Last time I emailed you and told you everything that was going on in my life you answered with a thumbs-up emoji." I laughed and shook my head. "I couldn't believe it. I spilled my guts and that's how you responded."

"Come on," he said. "What did you expect?"

"You're right," I said. "I forgot who we were to each other. For a minute, I thought we were real friends. But you're just some guy I used to make out with in high school."

"I'm some guy you almost married," he said. "I'm some guy who gave you your first orgasm."

"No," I said. "I gave myself my first orgasm. Granted, I was with you, but that's beside the point."

I heard a mallard squawk. We both looked toward the water.

"Arizona has mallard ducks?" Tom asked. "That seems odd."

"I think they're everywhere in the U.S.," I said, "but they remind me of Michigan. How's your family? Everyone doing well?"

He nodded. "Emily is finishing her first year of college. She likes it."

"How's your wife?" I asked. "Wait. Or is she your ex-wife? I've lost track." I grinned. "What is it with you, Tommy? You seem to go back and forth between the same women."

"It's easier," he said. "Otherwise I have to learn new names. The names of new family members. What positions she likes. Keep it to two, and I'm doing all right. Besides, if you and I had gotten married that would have stuck."

"You old romantic," I said. "We would have never 'stuck!' You liked hanging out with your buddies drinking and getting high more than you liked being with me. I bet you anything that's what drives your wife crazy about you. And you wanted to stay in that little town and I wanted to see the world."

He shrugged and put his thumb up. I laughed. "Funny, funny guy."

"My wife doesn't think we have anything in common," he said. "I don't really get that. What more do we have to have in common? We live in the same place, we have a kid together. We've been together for a long time. By the way, she still brings up those months I lived in Oregon when you and Jake were separated."

"Come on," I said. "She has to know you didn't move out there for me."

He bit into his burrito again and didn't look at me.

"Tom, you've never changed a bit of your life for anyone but you."

"Hey, I flew all the way out to Arizona to see if you were OK. Flying nowadays ain't exactly a ball of fun."

"I thought you had work out here," I said. "I mean, that's why you came last year."

He looked at me.

"You mean you didn't?"

"I know it's been rough for you moving here," he said. "I thought you could use a friend."

"Or a fuck buddy?"

"Or a fuck buddy," he said. "I'm open for that."

"Man. I'm sorry. I sound so mean and cranky. My daughter was giving me a hard time for having lunch with you. Even Jake seemed a little off about it."

"And why not?" Tom said. "Look at me. I'm a catch. Who wouldn't want to run off with me?"

"Who said anything about running off with you," I said. "Are you proposing we run off?"

"Hey, I know you love your husband. He's a good guy having a rough time. You've stood by him. Except for those few months when you left him." He smiled. "When you got my hopes up. But if you want to run off now, say to my hotel, I'd be game for that."

"Eat your lunch," I said.

"Can't blame a guy for asking," he said. "Seriously though, are things better?"

"Jake seems better," I said. "He's been sober for a few years. He's got his real estate license. and he's making a little money. I've been taking tourists out to see birds. That is not a huge income stream. I am probably gonna have to go back to work, and I don't want to work with the public any more. I don't want to be around people."

Tom leaned toward me. "Now you understand how I feel," he said. "People suck. I've always thought that. Unless they're offering me a beer. Then they're OK."

I knew he didn't believe that. He had always gotten along with people. They liked him. Because he was a good old boy who never questioned anything. And I never fit with him. In high school, they all thought we would get married and live happily ever after, the football captain and the vice president of our graduating class. But I couldn't do it. It felt suffocating. It felt small. I wanted something different.

That was then.

Now I thought maybe small would be OK. Maybe the same would be all right, too.

I imagined Tom and I going back to his motel. Taking our clothes off. Or maybe not. When we were kids, all we had to do was rub against each other. When we had been together a few years ago, it had been a little slower. But not by much. Something about being with your first love. Even if that love was not the love of your life.

"Jake is talking about getting a teaching job again," I said.

"That's a good thing, right? He can't be afraid forever."

"He's not afraid," I said. "Remember he went back to work right after the shooting for a while. I was the one who was terrified."

"The odds of something like that happening again are low," Tom said.

I shook my head. "I feel like it is all falling apart."

"Some might say it was never together."

"Easy for you. You're an almost-old white guy. It's all going fine for you. Meanwhile, the rest of us are getting our rights stripped one by one. And mostly white men are running around the country with guns killing people."

"I can't argue with that," Tom said. "But you can't stop having a life because of it."

"I have a life," I said. "It's stale. Or something. Like I'm waiting for the other shoe to drop."

"I get it," he said. "The whole world does seem to be out of whack. Guess we have to grab all the gusto we can when we can." He suddenly looked tired.

"Are you and your wife back together?" I asked.

"Naw," he said. "I think she finally had enough. Truth is I don't have much to say to her."

"Why?" I asked. "I bet you talk to your buddies nonstop."

"It's different," he said. "You talk to your buddies about shit that doesn't matter. And at home, you talk about shit that doesn't matter either and that takes up so much of your time. The toilet is leaking. The oil in the car needs changing. You know, that crap."

"Yes," I said. "It is exhausting."

"This is beautiful," Tom said as he looked around the park.

"I am thinking of coming down here for good. I do most of my work remotely now. What do you think?"

"Don't leave your friends and family to come here," I said. "Remember how lonely you were when you moved to Oregon for those months."

"I wasn't lonely," he said. "I don't think I get lonely."

I laughed. "You missed everyone and everything. Michigan is your home. Stay there. You've got community there."

"I don't have this weather there," Tom said.

"Get a condo then," I said, "and come down for part of the winter. But don't come here to live. I haven't met anyone here. I feel like my mom here. Like I've disappeared. Or I'm invisible."

"You don't go anywhere," Tom said. "That's why you're invisible. You think people are gonna come to you?"

"They better not," I said. "I don't want anyone I don't know on my property."

"I'm getting mixed signals from you."

"Don't you feel that way since the pandemic?" I asked. "Like everyone is dangerous? I felt that way after the shooting and then the pandemic made it even worse. Watching my kids and husband and myself for illness. Waiting to see every moment if we were gonna die. I hated it. And I still hate it. People are still getting sick every day."

"But it's better," Tom said.

"Is it?" I asked. "Isn't there another pandemic right around the corner? They haven't changed anything to stop it from happening again. Remember when we were kids we thought we could change the world? What have we done?"

"We changed the world," Tom said. "Think climate change."

"It's not funny, Tom."

"But I can't do anything about it," Tom said. "Do you want me to be unhappy 24 hours a day like you?"

"I'm not unhappy 24 hours a day," I said.

"You're not?"

I put my head down on the picnic table. The table shifted as Tom got up. He sat next to me and put his arm across my shoulders. I leaned against him and breathed deeply. I liked his smell. Was he still wearing Old Spice? Couldn't be. He smelled like himself. Only older. It would be so easy to go back to his hotel with him. Or take him to my house. And think about nothing except being together for a few minutes.

And that's all it would be: a few minutes. Then I would have to deal with the ramifications of those minutes. Because this time I wasn't separated. How would I explain it to Jake? Would he start drinking again? His drinking wasn't my responsibility, but wasn't it? We are responsible for how we treat each other. I wouldn't like it if Jake slept with his high school sweetheart.

Maybe all of this was old-fashioned. We had been through so much. What would it matter if I had a fling with Tom now?

I reached up and patted Tom on the cheek.

"Come on," I said. "Let's take a walk."

"I'd rather see your place," Tom said.

"Why?"

"You've been telling me how great your place is for years. Why not? You got something else to do?"

No, I didn't have anything else to do. My bird group for this afternoon had cancelled yesterday.

"OK," I said. "Why not?"

Tom stood and stretched. Then he leaned down and kissed me on the lips. A friendly peck. He began putting the used food wrappers into the takeout bag. I noticed an old blue Toyota pickup driving by then, on the other side of the line of palms. It looked like Jake's pickup, although so did a lot of other old blue Toyotas. And Jake wouldn't be here. Besides, he had taken the sedan this morning. Hadn't he?

I picked up my phone and looked at it. No new messages from him. The last one was soon after breakfast, telling me he made it to Vail and he was waiting for his clients.

"Someone you know in the truck?" Tom asked.

I shook my head. "I don't think so. Jake has a truck that looks like that," I said.

"Does he know you're here?" Tom asked.

"I can't remember if I told him or not," I said. "But Jake has never been jealous or possessive." Although he had never been a drunk either, until he was. "No. It ain't him."

Couldn't be.

Chapter Four

I drove down our long dirt drive and parked under the carport. I glanced toward the barn. Jake's car was there. I wondered why he was home. This could be awkward. He hadn't seen Tom in a long while, never laid eyes on him when Tom and I were dating during our separation. I glanced toward the barn. Jake's truck was gone.

I looked at my phone.

"Shit." I had it on airplane mode again. It was a new phone, and I kept pressing the wrong icons. I tapped it back on. I glanced up. Tom's rented SUV was coming down the drive. My phone beeped. A text message. From Jake. "I decided to take the truck. FYI." It was before the text about being in Vail. Stupid phone.

I quickly typed: "Had lunch w/ Tom at Agua Caliente. Showing him the property. Looking forward to pizza. Love."

I got out of my car as Tom parked his.

I looked down at my phone. No return text from Jake. I hoped he wouldn't be upset about Tom being here. He had always been a laid-back guy. At least before the shooting. Now it was as if I had to learn his ways all over again. Ways that kept changing. It had been years since the shooting, and everything and everyone still felt up in the air.

I married a steady guy. I wanted my steady guy back.

I wondered why he had come back for the truck. Could that have been him at Agua Caliente Park? Why would he have gone there? He hadn't known I was meeting Tom there, did he? Unless he was checking my phone. Unless I mentioned it and couldn't remember it now.

I put my phone in my pocket as Tom walked up to me.

"This is like your own little ranch," he said. "Do you have any animals?"

"We have lots of wild animals," I said. "Bobcats, badgers, cottontails, rattlesnakes, pack rats, mice, lizards, javelinas, and so many birds."

"Lions and tigers and bears."

"Oh my," I said. "We have water stations all over the property, to help out the wild things when it's hot and dry."

"Isn't that all the time?"

"Pretty much," I said. "The people who built the place had horses. We talked about getting a couple, for the kids, but they decided against it."

"Why?"

"Horse slavery, mostly," I said.

Tom laughed. "Really?"

"Well, I told the kids they would be completely responsible for taking care of the horses and making certain they were happy and healthy. Once they understood the work that entailed, they lost interest."

Tom laughed. "You don't use the barn at all?"

"It has a little apartment in it," I said. "It's mostly used as Jake's office. He goes there when he's having trouble sleeping.

On the other side, where the horse stalls are, is gardening equipment. I keep trying to grow veggies. Mostly, I kill plants."

"You can't see any neighbors," he said. "That's nice. There are a lot more trees here than I would have expected."

"A couple of washes run through the property," I said, "turning into streams for a short time during the monsoons. Tucson used to have rivers running through it all year long and our aquifer water met up with the ground water, so trees could thrive. But pumping has pretty much devastated the whole area. The trees have died or are dying. Too many people, too many developers, too much agriculture. Developers and big AG are bosses in this area, and they do whatever they want."

"That's true everywhere now, I think," Tom said. "Remember Livingston County was the fastest growing county in the U.S. when we were growing up."

"I hated that," I said. "People ruin everything."

"You wouldn't recognize it now," he said. "It's so crowded. So many cars and people. Wish you would visit now and again."

"No reason to now that Dad is gone, too."

He glanced at me.

"No, I'm not going all the way back to Michigan to see my high school sweetheart. That wouldn't make anyone happy."

"Aren't some of your sisters still there?"

"Two of them live near Detroit," I said, "but we don't have anything in common. And since the shooting and the pandemic, it feels like a lot of work."

"Don't you have a sister in Phoenix, too?" he asked.

"We don't talk," I said. "She's never even been out here. She thought I was 'too negative' during the pandemic." I put up quote fingers when I said negative. "As it was starting, I said it would be bad, and we all needed to take steps to be safe, and she didn't want to hear it. She wanted to ignore it all."

"Isn't she a nurse?" Tom asked.

"Yep."

We walked under two eucalyptus trees to the Big Corral. The Big Corral looked like a small field now, covered in tiny blue and yellow and red wildflowers.

"This was empty when we came," I said. "The first owners had their horses out here. By the time we bought the place it was where rabbits came to poop pretty much. I wanted our seed birds to have an open space, and I wanted some wildflowers. So I seeded the field. We didn't get much last year—I think the curve-billed thrashers ate the seeds—but look at it this year."

"It's nice," Tom said.

I laughed. "Nice? It's beautiful."

"Sure," Tom said. "If you like flowers."

"Even if you don't like flowers, it's lovely. It's OK to say so. Your testicles aren't gonna shrivel up or anything."

"Already shriveled," he said.

Tom leaned against the fence that surrounded the field. "It is pretty, but isn't it a waste of space? Why not a food garden? Or a baseball field for Jules to practice on."

"Not only is this pretty to look at," I said, "but these are all native flowers, so the pollinators love them: birds, butterflies, bees. They evolved with the native flowers and the flowers evolved with them, so it all works."

Tom put his arm across my waist and hugged me for a moment. "I like hearing the excitement in your voice. You sound like you again."

"It is nice to help create something," I said. "To help something grow. To provide water and know it's helping the wildlife."

"You created two kids," Tom said. "That's more than I could do. You know, because I'm a man. I provided the sperm. Margaret had to do all the work."

"Yep," I said. "Having little parasites inside you for nine months each is pretty creative."

"What?"

"I love my kids. I'm glad they're here in the world, but I didn't like being pregnant. I was sick the whole time, and then I was depressed afterward. I've never been one of these parents who had to be with my kids all the time. I liked going to work. I liked talking to adults. But then after the shooting, I could barely stand them out of my sight. That has gotten better. Probably because they are both teenagers, which is exhausting. I can't wait until they grow up and go away. Especially my daughter. I really don't like her."

"Mom!"

Tom dropped his arm from my waist, and I turned around. Jules was standing ten feet away.

Crap. Had she heard me? She glared at me, but that wasn't unusual.

"What are you doing home?" I asked. I would pretend she hadn't heard. Or seen. Put her on the defensive.

She looked at Tom who watched us both.

"You remember Tom Kelly," I said. "Tom, my daughter Jules."

She didn't acknowledge him.

"I've been calling and texting you and Dad," she said.

"You have?" I pulled my phone out of my back pocket. I had put it on airplane mode again. What was wrong with me? I took it off. I heard it beep several times, indicating incoming messages.

"How did you get home?"

"Daisy lent me her car."

Ten messages from Jules. I tried to read them. Jules interrupted me. "Colin Moore escaped!"

"What are you talking about?" I asked.

She held her phone out to me. It was open to a breaking news story on Oregon Live: "School Shooter Colin Moore At Large." I tried to read the story, but Jules took the phone away.

"Did you talk to your dad?" I asked.

"No! He didn't pick up," she said.

"OK, OK," I said. "I'll call him. I don't want him to hear about it on the news or by text."

"I already texted him!" Jules said. "I couldn't get a hold of you. Where were you? I thought he should know."

"I was at lunch," I said.

"I called you before," she said. "Why didn't you pick up?"

"Before lunch?" I said. "I got some groceries. I-I didn't get any calls."

"Or else you were ignoring me," she said.

"I wouldn't ignore you," I said. Not in the middle of the day.

"There could have been a school shooter," she said. "It could have been my last call to you, and you ignored me!"

"Stop it, Jules," I said. "I didn't ignore you. It's a new phone. I don't know what I'm doing with it."

"You don't know what you're doing period!" she said. "That killer could be on his way down here to get Dad. Or us."

I rubbed my face. "Let me find out what's going on," I said, "but he's not coming down here. He doesn't know where we are. And even if he did, he has no reason to come after us."

"He's insane!" Jules said. "Reason has nothing to do with it." She looked terrified. I started to put my arms around her, but she moved away.

"I better get going," Tom said. "Unless you want me to stick around."

"No," I said. "I need to figure this out. I'll get a hold of you later."

We gave each other a quick hug. He squeezed my arm. "Give my regards to Jake," he said quietly. He hurried away. I looked around. Jules was headed to the house. I followed her. I immediately called our lawyer in Oregon. I stood on the back patio, under the overhang in front of the pool. I squinted, trying to see everything I could from every direction.

"Stephanie, why didn't someone call us and tell us he escaped?" I asked when she finally answered.

"I just found out," Stephanie said. "No one told me. You're not considered a victim, so they wouldn't call you. I don't even know if they'd call Horace's family."

It sounded weird to hear her call him Horace instead of Mr. Miller. She hadn't known him.

"What happened?" I asked. "I thought he was in prison! People don't escape from prison."

"Not as a rule," she said. "But he was showing signs of mental illness, so he was sent to a psychiatric unit, and then he got ill. Might have been COVID. I think they weren't watching him closely enough. You know, skinny little white boy. And he escaped. He was gone a few hours before they noticed."

"You're kidding me?"

"I wish I were," she said. "But your family has nothing to fear. Remember he said he liked Jake."

"He liked Mr. Miller, too!" I said. "And he killed him!"

"You're so far away," she said. "He wouldn't know how to find you. And even if he did, it would take days to get down there. He has no ID. He can't get on a plane."

"Jake is a real estate agent," I said. "Anyone could google him and find him."

She was silent for a moment. "That's true," she said. "But the police have assured the public they are not in danger."

I laughed. "Meaningless," I said. "Fucking meaningless. I'm surprised the president hasn't pardoned him yet. I mean he only killed a black man and then tried to kill a brown man because some woman wouldn't go out with him. He's an incel hero!" I took a deep breath. "When did he escape?"

"Last night," she said. "They think."

"Fuck," I said. "That means he could be here tonight if he drove straight through."

"He's not coming to find you," Stephanie said. "He's probably got a girlfriend somewhere. I'll let you know if I hear anything. I gotta go into court. Talk to you soon."

I called Jake's phone next. It rang and rang. I texted him: "Call me as soon as you get this."

I called his work.

The receptionist answered. "Hi, Gabby," I said to her. "I'm looking for Jake."

"Hello, Mrs. Acosta," she said.

I didn't correct her. I was not Mrs. Acosta. His mother was.

"I haven't seen Jake today. Let me look at his schedule. He was showing a house in Vail. He checked in after that and said he was heading out for the day. Let me see if anyone else has seen him."

"He's meeting with Stuart later," I said. "Could I talk with him?"

"Let me check."

And she was gone. I listened to silence. One minute. Two minutes. Three.

"Are you still there?" Gabby asked. "Stuart isn't here. I checked his schedule, and it looks like he was having lunch with Jake. It doesn't say where."

"Oh," I said. I thought he was meeting Stuart later at Lucy's. "OK. Thank you. If you hear from Jake or Stuart, will you have them call me?"

"I will. Is everything all right?"

"Everything is fine," I said. "Have a good day."

I called Stuart next. Jake had given me his private number

soon after he went to work there. It rang once and then went to a message. "Hello, Stuart." I had only met him once briefly. He wouldn't remember my name. "I'm Jake Acosta's wife, and I need to get ahold of him ASAP. Please call me when you get this or if you're with Jake, have him call me." And I left my number.

"Mom!" Jules called from the house. "It's all over the news."

I went into the house. Jules stood in the living room watching the TV.

"Go get your brother," I said. "I think I know where your father is. Let's meet back here. Keep the doors locked."

"Why? Do you think Colin is coming for us?" Jules asked.

"No!" I said. "I lock the doors. You know that."

We left the house together. I locked the door and double-checked it. Jules left in Daisy's car first, and then I followed in mine. I hoped Jake hadn't read any of Jules' messages, and I hoped to find him with Stuart at Lucy's, without a drink in hand.

Chapter Five

It took me 20 minutes to find Lucy's. In Tucson terms, it was close by. It was in a kind of strip mall with a huge parking lot. I looked around for Jake's truck, but I didn't see it.

I walked into Lucy's. I waited a few moments for my vision to adjust to the relative darkness. The place was packed with diners. It smelled like a mixture of burgers, tacos, and beer. I really wished I had worn a mask.

"Where are you, Jake?" I whispered. "Jake, Jake, Jake."

I spotted Stuart then, across the restaurant, sitting at a table with two other men. At least I thought it was him. He looked up and saw me, seemed to recognize me. He waved and got up and came across the room.

"Hello," I said when he reached me. "I need to speak to Jake." No niceties. I needed to find Jake.

"He was supposed to meet me here half an hour ago," he said. "He didn't show up, and I can't get a hold of him."

My stomach tightened.

"He mentioned to me he was meeting you, but I thought it was later in the day."

He nodded. "I had Gabby change the time. Something came up."

"Are you sure Jake got the message?" I asked.

"I assumed so," he said. "Gabby called and left a message and texted him."

"Do you know if he answered her?" I asked.

"I assumed so."

"Sometimes he misplaces his phone."

"That's true," Stuart said. "I didn't think of that. Can I talk to you about something? Outside?"

"Sure," I said.

He opened the door, and I went through it and outside. He touched my elbow and moved me away from the door and other people. I didn't like him touching me.

"Has anything been going on with Jake?" he asked.

"What do you mean?" I asked. "No. Everything's fine. Why?"

"You know Jake takes the deposit to the bank on the days he's in the office."

"No, I didn't know," I said. "But I don't know the details of his work." Going to the bank didn't sound like a job for a realtor.

"The bank is on his way home," Stuart said. "It saves me or Gabby some time. Tuesday deposit never made it to the bank."

Today was Thursday.

I blinked.

"And?"

"Jake was supposed to take it to the bank," Stuart said.

"Did you ask him about it on Wednesday?"

"No," Stuart said. "We didn't know that it never got there until today. He took the deposit on Wednesday."

"And it got to the bank?" I asked. "All was well with it?"

"Yes," he said.

"You're a realty company," I said. "People buy and sell houses. You're not a cash business. It can't be a big deal. Ask him about it. Jake has never stolen anything in his life. And he wouldn't steal anything!"

"I know you've been having some cash flow problems," he said.

My head began to pound. Where was Jake? I did not want to have this conversation with a stranger.

"We are not having cash flow problems," I said. "Talk to Jake about it. He spaces things out every once in a while."

"Because of his panic attacks?" Stuart asked.

I looked at him. Jake had told him about those?

"Yes," I said.

Stuart looked around. "Normally you're right. There's not a lot of cash. But on Tuesday, there was a cash deposit of ten thousand dollars."

"The deposit that is missing had ten thousand dollars in it?" I asked.

Jesus H.

"Oh my gawd," I said. "That's awful. But-but Jake wouldn't have taken it."

"Of course not, of course not," Stuart said. "But he was the last person to have it. So I've got to talk to him. We've got to figure it out."

"Maybe the bank made a mistake," I said. Yes, that was it.

"Of course," Stuart said. He was agreeing with me, but he was shaking his head.

"I am telling you on the life of my children that Jake would not have taken that money," I said. "If it got misplaced or lost or something, I will make certain it is—it is replaced. But I'm sure there's an innocent explanation about the deposit. And Jake not showing up for lunch: He probably never got the change of time. What time was it, originally."

"Three-thirty," he said.

Two hours from now.

"But I can't be here then," he said. "That's why I changed the time."

I nodded. I wasn't going to sit around here for two hours to see if he'd show up. I needed to find Jake now.

"I'll catch up with him," I said. "I'm sure it's a big mistake. I promise. It'll be fine."

Stuart didn't look convinced.

"I hope he's all right," he said. "I know it's been a difficult time."

"A difficult time?" It had been a difficult time for years. Why would now be different?

"Because of the anniversary."

Our anniversary wasn't until—Oh. The anniversary of the shooting. Fuck, fuck, fuck.

"He said these blue mornings remind him of that day. Because it was such a beautiful morning that day."

I put my hands over my eyes.

"I'm sorry," he said. "I shouldn't have brought it up."

I shook my head. "No. No, it's fine. I'll find out about the deposit and get back with you. It'll be OK. It'll be OK."

Stuart nodded. "I know it will be. Don't worry."

Too late, too late, too fucking late.

"Here's my card," he said. "Call me if you hear anything."

I hurried away from him to my car. I got in, closed the door, locked it, and pulled out my phone.

No messages from Jake.

I stared at the phone and then screamed, "What the fuck, Jake? What the holy fuck?"

How could he be so irresponsible? First not to keep in touch with me. But to lose ten thousand dollars? Because he didn't steal it. Jesus. That was ridiculous.

Unless he got drunk. Could he have gotten drunk on Tuesday, before he went to the bank, and did something with the money?

I shook my head and closed my eyes.

No. No. I would have known.

I had taken a group of birders out to the San Pedro River on Tuesday morning. When I got home, Jake had been sitting on the patio, looking out at the desert, his hand wrapped around a glass of tea.

At least I thought it was tea.

He had smiled when he saw me. Got up and kissed me. Long and deep. Like old times. But when I reached down, he wasn't hard. And I pulled away from him.

He took my hand. "Come on," he said, "maybe if we go to the bedroom. Maybe if we work on it."

I pulled my hand from his.

"I have to work at everything," I said. "I don't want to work at fucking."

"I can pleasure you," he said.

I grimaced. I knew it wasn't his fault. It was all wrapped up in the trauma. Doctors said he was healthy. Ready to go. But it felt humiliating to me. Like I wasn't good enough. Sexy enough.

It made me feel like we were both broken and would never be fixed.

"I miss the old Jake," I said, "the Jake who got a hard-on if I brushed past him in the hallway."

"I miss him, too," he said.

"I'm sorry. I shouldn't have said that."

He nodded. "I'll go pick up the kids."

But later, after the kids were asleep, or at least after their doors were shut, we closed our door, took off our clothes, and it all worked. We made love. Took a little effort, but it was OK. It was good. It was . . . sex.

We fell asleep in each other's arms. Which was nice. When I awakened in the middle of the night, I sat up and stared down at him. In his sleep, he looked so young, like the person I had met in college. I wanted to kiss his mouth, have him wrap me in his arms, wanted to kiss his nipples, and watch and feel him get harder and harder. I ran my fingers across his bare chest. He made a noise and turned away from me in his sleep.

Sometimes it felt like the shooting had killed all of his desire, his joy, his pleasure. Although maybe it had nothing to do with the shooting. Maybe he didn't love me anymore. Didn't seem like he wanted me. At least his body didn't. The shooting had crushed my joy, too, but it had made me want to hold those I loved closer. And closer. Even when they pulled away from me.

Now I started the car. I looked around again, in case Jake had showed up. No truck. No Jake.

I hurried home. The kids were there. Daisy's car was gone; she must have brought them back. Daisy was Jules' girlfriend, but we hardly ever saw her. Jules said she was shy. I didn't know the truth of it. Wished we could know her better. Mattie hadn't started to date—at least as far as I knew. He preferred going out with a group of people. It was all fine with me. As long as they stayed in touch with us.

They both sat on the couch, phone in hand, the TV on, muted. I wanted to sit on the couch with them and hold them, pet them, never let them go.

"There's nothing new," Jules said. "He escaped last night. He hasn't gone to his parents or his girlfriend's house. Can you imagine? He has a girlfriend? What must her self-esteem be like?"

"Why would someone date a murderer?" Mattie asked, not looking up. "It's not like she wouldn't know. He's in prison."

"You two need a snack?" I asked.

Mattie shook his head. Jules didn't answer.

"Have you called your dad?" I asked.

"He doesn't answer," Jules said. "It rings and rings."

"Maybe the phone is here," I said. "Maybe he forgot it."

I called his phone and walked around the house, listening for the ring, watching for the vibration in case he had turned the sound off. I didn't hear it in the house or find it anywhere.

"I'm going to check the apartment," I said. "Will one of you call your grandparents and see if he's there?"

"I'll do it," Mattie said.

I called Jake's number again as I stepped out of the house. I walked into the barn. I pressed my face against the passenger window of his car, but I didn't see or hear a phone. I went into the unlocked apartment—I'd have to talk to him about leaving it unlocked. I called the number again. Didn't hear it. The bed was made. His desk was neat and cleared except for one pile of papers. I went around the desk and flipped through the papers. Mostly notes on various houses that were for sale. His desk calendar was open to today. He had the initials S.H. scribbled on it.

S.H. Who was that? No time attached to it. It wasn't Stuart. His last name was Bowman. Or something with a B. I flipped the pages forward. Tomorrow was clear. And the next day. And the next. He didn't have anything else written on any calendar day going forward. I flipped to dates in the past. Almost every day had something written on it. On Tuesday, he had a star drawn in the right hand corner. That was the day the deposit was never made. It was the night we had sex, but I never knew him to mark our times of intimacy on a calendar. I used to do that when I was younger and trying either to get pregnant or not get pregnant. It also seemed unlikely that he would star the time he forgot to make a deposit.

Or the time he stole ten thousand dollars.

That was not anywhere in the realm of possibilities.

I left the apartment and locked the door behind me. I hadn't brought the keys to Jake's car, but I tried the driver's door. It was unlocked. I popped the trunk. I had seen too many crime shows not to pop the trunk and make certain nothing was inside it. I went around to the open trunk. It was clean and empty.

I hurried back into the house, locking the door behind me. The kids were still on the couch.

"Grandma and Grandpa have not seen or heard from Dad," Mattie said. "At least Grandma doesn't think so. Grandpa was out back digging another hole, but she'll ask him when he comes back."

"No one finds buried treasure in their own back yard," I said. "Now he wants to dig holes on our property. I keep telling him no one has ever been here who had any kind of treasure."

"Everyone has their thing," Jules said. "That's his thing."

I heard my phone. I looked down. It was a text from Stephanie. "No news on where CM is."

I had to find Jake and let him know what was going on.

Unless he already knew. Unless he had read Jules' texts and they had freaked him out and he had gone to a bar and gotten drunk. Or bought drugs somewhere. Or had a panic attack.

And where was the money?

"Jake, please call me," I whispered.

Suddenly I remembered Jules' baseball game.

"Don't you need to get ready for your game?" I asked.

"I'm not going," she said.

"What?"

"I told them I had a family emergency," she said. "So I'll miss a game. No big deal."

"Aren't they counting on you?"

She looked up from her phone. "They'll be fine without me, Mom. Are you trying to get rid of me? I thought you'd be happy that I was putting family first."

"Is that what's really going on or did you want to skip a game?"

"I don't have to put up with this shit." Jules got up and started to stomp out of the room.

"You need to stay here," I said.

"Which is it, Mom? Stay here or go? Make up your mind!" She screamed the last part.

"Stay here," I said. "Let's all stay here. Dad will be home soon."

"How do you know?" Mattie asked.

"She doesn't know," Jules said, plopping down on the couch again. "For all she knows—for all anyone knows—he is gone for good."

Chapter Six

"Wait," I said. "Wait, wait, wait." I was thinking about all of this from a place of trauma. I had to look at it differently, from the viewpoint of someone who hadn't experienced what we had. Jake was out and about in town somewhere. Nothing bad or tragic was going on now. Jake was going to meet us at the game. So Jules needed to go to the game, and we would see Jake there.

I wished I could call my mother or father. Wished they had been people I could have called when I needed advice when they were alive, but they weren't. They didn't want to hear about any trying times. Grin and fucking bear it, whatever it was, and whatever you do, do not disturb their peace—because it wasn't actually peaceful. My mother was trying to get by in spite of her illnesses. It was probably more my father than my mother who didn't want to hear anything that might be upsetting. I could almost understand this nowadays. Because remembering all the bad shit certainly didn't make it better.

Right now though, right this second, I was falling into catastrophic thinking before I knew if there was a catastrophe or not.

I mean, I couldn't get a hold of Jake for a couple hours. So what? When I was younger, my parents could be gone all day, and I wouldn't know when they were coming home. I didn't worry. At least, I didn't think I did. I worried all the time about other things, but I don't think I was afraid they wouldn't return.

Jake had probably lost his phone. He had probably put that deposit in the bank, and they somehow screwed it up. And murderous Colin Moore didn't care anything about us and wasn't looking for us.

I breathed deeply. Yes, that was it. I should know better. I was making a mountain out of a molehill as my mom used to say. It was all a molehill.

"Jules," I said, "your dad was going to meet us at the game. If you want to play, why don't you go ahead. We'll all go."

Jules looked at her brother.

"Colin Moore is several states away," I said. "Even if he's coming here—which he's not—he's not going to arrive any time soon. Let's act normal. Be normal."

Jules looked like she wanted to say something—something smart ass, I was certain. Something about us not being normal. But she didn't. She nodded. "I was looking forward to the game."

"OK," I said. "You can take Dad's car. Take Mattie with you. You guys can stop somewhere and get something to eat. We'll get pizza afterward. We'll all have dinner together. It'll be nice. It'll be good."

The kids agreed. No one argued. They wanted everything to be all right, too. At that moment, I had convinced myself that Jules had overreacted and I had stupidly followed her lead. Not that I was blaming her. Her constant wheedling threw me off-balance. Did that happen to all mothers of teenagers, or was I a clueless mom? A bad mom?

I didn't have the time or inclination to go down that road. I called Jake's work again, hoping to talk to Gabby and find out if Jake had acknowledged the change in lunch time with Stuart. No one answered. It went to voice mail after four rings.

I texted Tom. "Things are calming down here. Still no Jake. We'll talk later."

He sent a thumbs-up emoji. I laughed. "Good to know, Tom."

The kids left—after Mattie kissed me goodbye. Jules waved.

"Be careful," I said, as I always did.

"I'll save you and Dad a seat." Mattie.

"Thanks, love."

Then they were gone. The house throbbed with silence. I sat on the couch and put my head in my hands. I had to stop thinking something was wrong if I didn't hear from one of them for five minutes. It was so fucking exhausting. Or if one of them sneezed or coughed, I was sure they had COVID or some new deadly virus. It was hard on the kids, and it was hard on me.

The morning of the shooting had been perfect. I hated that almost more than anything. I wished we had been cranky with each other. Wished I had stubbed my toe or the kids had been fighting. But none of that happened.

Instead, Jake and I had awakened at the same time to a quiet house. The kids were still sleeping. We wrapped our legs and arms around one another and held on tightly, giggling and whispering sweet nothings to each other as we made love. Nothing in the world felt as good as being in Jake's arms. Nothing in the world felt as good as his lips on my skin. He would breathe deeply, as though he were drinking me in, and he was—in a way—because he loved my smell, especially if I was a little sweaty or I had been outside in the woods. "You smell like nature," he'd say. "Earthy." He loved that I was myself, wild and unperfumed, unpainted, as Nature made me.

When I was a girl, my wild child personality did not go over well with my mother. They practically pinned me down and put a bra on me when I was twelve. I hated it. Felt like I was a horse in a harness: and everyone could see that harness. Now I was like all the other girls, forced to hide my body from boys because, you know, you don't want to excite the boys because they might hurt you. "Then fix the boys!" I wanted to scream.

As soon as I was old enough, I took the harness off, and I never let anyone again tell me how I had to look or dress or talk to be a woman.

This often meant I got along with more men than women. I saw women as my sisters. We were together in the struggle against the patriarchy. It made me laugh to think about it now. I may have thought all those things, but I didn't find any women who considered themselves my sisters in the "struggle against the patriarchy."

After I had kids and started interacting with parents in school, I began dressing more the part: brushed my hair, wore layers so they wouldn't know I wasn't wearing a bra, pinched my cheeks so they looked rosy. Didn't bring up the patriarchy at school meetings. Of course, it was Oregon, so I didn't have to change much about myself to be just one of the parents.

And working at a public library made me a little invisible. The Great Unwashed needed a place to stay, and others wanted me to point the way to whatever book or information they needed. My looks, my voice, my self was not important or encouraged. We were public servants. We were to act the part: servile.

Jake was noticed everywhere he went. He was a gorgeous brown-skinned man in Portland, OR, where pale white was the norm. He was gregarious, friendly, a great storyteller. When he looked at you, he seemed to actually see you. All the men wanted to be his friend, and all the women wanted to fuck him. Probably some of the men wanted to fuck him, too.

And that morning, the morning of the shooting, we made love, quietly, quickly, before the kids got up, and it was lovely. I still remembered it. I guess the trauma imprinted everything on my memory from that day.

Afterward, Jake made pancakes for the kids. The kitchen smelled of blueberries and maple syrup. Sugary. And the kids laughed and laughed—at least that's how I remembered it. Jake kept telling bad dad jokes. Knock knock jokes.

The four of us had gone outside for a few minutes to listen to the birds. The sky was so blue. The air was clear and clean. We stood under our huge old Doug fir, the four of us, our arms around each other. Jake had one arm across my waist; he held Mattie's hand with his other hand, and I had my arm across Jules' shoulders. We were smiling and laughing. We liked each other. It was perfect. It was the family I never had when I was a kid. I was able to do that for Jules and Mattie, and it was working. It was working for all of us. I was loved, liked, and cherished, too. Isn't that what everyone wanted?

Then Jake drove the kids to their schools and went on to his, and I walked a few blocks to the library where I worked. Jake texted, "Got to school. Beautiful day. Wish you were here. Love."

It wasn't long after before Jenine asked me if I had heard about the school shooting. I said, "I'm so sick of these shootings. What is wrong with this country?"

She said, "It was here. In Portland." She said the name of the school.

I may have screamed. I probably didn't. But in my memory, I heard a long low scream. Or groan. I ran to find my phone in the staff lounge—that was before I carried it everywhere. Nothing from Jake. I called him. It went straight to voice mail.

I didn't tell anyone anything. I ran out of the library and down the street. Raced home. It was still morning. The sky was still blue. The light on the street was dappled, even though the trees had not leafed out completely, but it was almost as though those old Portland trees were holding me, encouraging me, leading me home.

Why didn't Jake phone? Jake, Jake, Jake.

Time stood still. It seemed to take forever to know whether my world was over or not.

I got home. Ran up onto our porch. The phone rang. It was Jake. He was alive.

He was alive.

He was alive.

"Everything is OK," he said. "I'm all right."

But of course he wasn't.

My phone rang now and pulled me out of the past. It was Stephanie.

"Hey, Steph. Did they catch him?"

"No," she said. "Apparently his girlfriend gave him her car. The police are still talking to her. Maybe she'll tell them where he's going."

"The kids were wondering what kind of woman has a murderer for a boyfriend," I said, "after the fact."

"Have you seen her?" Stephanie asked.

"No."

"She's Black."

"What the fuck?"

"Yep," Stephanie said. "She says he's changed. He's no longer a white supremacist."

I laughed. It wasn't a very cheery laugh. Colin's lawyer had claimed he was crazy and not a racist at his trial. But he had killed a Black man—Mr. Miller—and tried to kill a brown one—Jake Acosta. He had a confederate flag draped over his bed, although in Oregon lots of people had confederate flags. It didn't mean they were all racist killers. I guess. Colin's traitorous flag was framed by three swastikas, so his lawyer's claims went nowhere.

"I talked to the police," Stephanie said.

"Oh, good," I said. "I figured Jake and I would call them tonight."

"I asked if they thought Jake and your family were in any danger," she said. "I reminded them that Jake had testified against Colin. Which would have been particularly galling to someone who hates immigrants."

"Jake isn't an immigrant," I said.

I could almost hear her roll her eyes. "My ancestors came here on slave ships hundreds of years ago and Colin Moore still considers me an immigrant. You know what I mean."

I sighed. "I know. I'm sorry. It's a knee-jerk reaction from when we lived in Oregon. I should get over it."

"Anyway. I talked to Detective Reese. You remember her. She didn't think Colin has enough intact marbles to figure out where you are. She said he's loonier than a flock of loonies."

I felt this irrational urge to defend loons and tell her that loons weren't crazier than any other bird, but then I realized my desire to correct people came from my desire to scream "you are all assholes!" when I was under stress.

"That is good news, I think," I said. "But it'll be better news if he runs into a tree at high speed and is killed. Not good news for the tree, but you get my point."

"Yep. I get it."

She sounded uncomfortable. Most good people were uncomfortable when someone else was wishing another someone else dead.

"Thanks, Stephanie. Let's keep in touch."

In one version of Jake's recurring dream, Jake grabs the barrel of the gun. Just as he had in real life. But in the dream, he smashes the butt of the gun into Colin's face again and again. Until he kills him.

He always awakened from that version moaning and crying. I'd hold him until he'd fall back asleep.

I liked that version of the dream. I liked imagining Colin dead. I wished he was dead. He had killed what peace my family had. Killed it dead. I thought the same should happen to him. People talked about forgiveness and having compassion for such a troubled person.

Bullshit. Bullshit. Bullshit.

After any of these mass shootings, I heard the same arguments again and again. "Get rid of guns." Yeah, OK, that would be great, but it wasn't gonna happen. "Do something about mental health." OK. Great, but that wasn't gonna happen either. The politicians weren't gonna fix it because they liked having this particular football. What they should be talking about was why our culture breeds these mostly white boys who believed they were entitled to kill every time something didn't go their way. Privileged entitled assholes raised mostly by entitled privileged assholes.

What had happened to our world where people were not even ashamed of their prejudices anymore? And now our political leaders were encouraging white men to be violent toward women and people of color and immigrants.

It pissed me off to no end.

A few months before the shooting, Jules and Mattie told us they wanted to change their last names. Jake explained that in his culture—in Mexico—children had their mother's and their father's name, just like our kids did. They didn't care. They lived in Oregon, they said. They wanted one last name.

We said, "Fine. You choose."

They wanted their dad's last name: Acosta.

"Your name is so white bread," Jules said.

"And Dad's name is first in the alphabet," Mattie said.

Jake was glad they were proud of their Mexican heritage. It never occurred to anyone that my feelings might be hurt. I thought, "This must be how Mom felt as she slowly disappeared from the world."

I told myself at the time that I was being silly. My last name had been my father's last name. It didn't really have that much meaning. Except it was mine. And I was their mother. Why didn't my name matter? I wondered if they even knew my first name. I asked them, and they both said, "Mom!" And then they laughed and ran away.

My mother once told me she thought all children had a little monster in them. I couldn't argue with that conclusion. Even though I loved my little (now big) monsters.

Soon after the shooting, Jake woke me up one night pacing the room. He was in a cold sweat. I asked him what was wrong. He came and sat on the edge of the bed next to me.

"The kids changed their name to Acosta," he said. "Now everyone will know they have Mexican heritage."

"So?" I said.

"Colin Moore tried to kill me because he thought I was a Mexican immigrant," he said.

I didn't know what to say. "Killers be stupid," were the words that came out.

"What's happening in the world is terrifying," he said. "There's so much backlash against people of color. Against immigrants. You can't understand. You're white."

"I can't understand?" I said. "Jesus, Jake. That's the stupidest thing you've ever said. I'm a fucking woman! They are systematically stripping away any rights women have over our own bodies. Everywhere we go we have to be aware. We can't relax. We can't let our guards down. Because it's not only assholes with guns who are after us. It's violent assholes everywhere who want us to disappear or to only cook and clean and fuck. So don't tell me I don't understand!"

He continued shaking or shivering, sweat beading off his forehead. Perhaps yelling at a man in the middle of a panic attack wasn't a good idea, but I could not let it pass. I had let so much pass in my life. But not this.

"Besides," I said, "no one knows Acosta is a surname in Mexico. And both of our children look very white no thanks to you."

I put my arm across his shoulders. He smiled. I wiped the sweat from his brow.

"It will be all right," I said, even though I didn't believe it.

Now I looked down at my phone. I wished Jake would call. It was almost time for his original meeting with Stuart. If Jake had lost his phone, he would go to Lucy's looking for Stuart. I should go there, too, on my way to the game, and intercept him.

"It will be all right," I told myself again. "It will be all right."

Chapter Seven

I was about to leave for Lucy's when someone pounded on our front door. My stomach did a flipflop. We didn't get visitors. I had made it pretty clear to friends and family since the pandemic that our house was off-limits. I had tried to make it a safe place for us. Of course my kids and husband saw people all day every day, so I didn't know how truly safe it was.

"It's Pedro!" I heard Jake's brother's voice.

Didn't want to let him in.

"Go around to the pool patio. I'll meet you."

I heard him grumble but then shuffle away.

We met under the overhang, out of the sun. I heard a fly-catcher calling out in the near distance. Ash-throated? Dusky-capped?

"Jake isn't here," I said.

"I figured," Pedro said. He was taller than Jake and stockier. "Mom told me you were looking for him. I tried calling him, but I didn't get through."

"I'm sure he lost his phone," I said. "He does that."

"Do you think he's out on a bender again?" Pedro asked. He had his hands on his hips. Like he had something to say.

"A bender?" I said. "No. He's been sober for a long time."

"Didn't he go missing last month?" Pedro asked.

"Missing? He misplaced his phone, and we didn't know where he was for a couple of hours. He was out showing a house."

"I don't want to be the one to tell you, but he's started drinking again."

"What are you talking about?" I said. "I would know. He would tell me."

Pedro rolled his eyes and shook his head. "Why would he tell you? Last time he was drinking you left him and ran off with another man."

"I did not run off with another man," I said. "It's none of your business, but Jake and I did separate for a few months when he couldn't get his shit together. He promised he would get sober and stay sober, and he has. He wouldn't lie to me."

"That's my point," he said. "You said you'd leave him if he drank again. He's not gonna fucking tell you he's drinking again."

"How do you know he's drinking?" I asked. "And how long's it been going on?"

"Since you moved back to Arizona," Pedro said.

I shook my head. I didn't believe it.

"I gotta go, Pedro. I don't have time to listen to your bullshit."

"I've sat next to him at the bar," Pedro said. "That's how I know."

I wanted to punch him.

"You know your brother is an alcoholic and you went to the bar and drank with him?"

"He's not an alcoholic," he said.

I groaned. "Of course he is. It runs in your family. Your father is an alcoholic."

Just like it ran in my family. My father was an alcoholic, and the last thing I ever wanted was a drunk for a husband.

Pedro shook his head. "No. My father was heartbroken. That's why he drank. Life, ya know. Now he's not heartbroken so he doesn't drink. Same with Jake. He's heartbroken so he drinks."

"You're gonna blame Jake's alcoholism on me? That's not how it works."

"He is heartbroken over what he saw," Pedro said. "Over what he couldn't stop. When he gets over that, he won't drink no more."

"Is that why you drink, Pedro? Are you heartbroken too?" I hoped he heard the sarcasm in my voice.

"I am," he said. "I pay attention. I know what's happening. My heart breaks every day. Doesn't yours?"

"Yes! But you don't see me lying to my family or hanging out at bars. I've got to go. Why did you come by?"

"I thought you should know," Pedro said. "I can look for him, if you want."

I crossed my fingers and then rubbed my face. I was so fucking tired.

"I don't care," I said.

I hurried out to my car, got in, started it, and drove too quickly down our dirt driveway. Headed to Lucy's. It couldn't be true. Jake would not do this to us. He might drink, yes; he was an alcoholic. They slip. But to hide it from us. I would have smelled it. Or him. Maybe he stopped at his brother's place after, to shower. To sober up. Still. I would have noticed something. Wouldn't I? Maybe that was why he couldn't get it up.

When I got to Lucy's, I looked for Jake's truck. Didn't see it.

I waited a few minutes, until it was past the time of his original appointment with Stuart. I kept checking my phone.

"Where the fuck are you, Jake?"

Nothing.

I went inside the bar and grill and looked around. The place was nearly empty. I walked over to the bar and sat on one of the stools. I hadn't been in a bar in years before today. Hadn't been inside a restaurant since the pandemic. A young woman came over and asked me what I wanted.

I had no idea.

Peace.

Truth.

The knowledge of where my fucking husband was.

"Do people still get screwdrivers?" I asked.

"I don't know about people," she said, sounding bored, "but I can make you one."

"To go," I said. I handed her a credit card. A couple minutes later, she handed me my card and a take-out cup I assumed was filled with orange juice and vodka.

"I threw in a little extra vodka," she said.

I pulled a couple dollars out of my wallet and put them on the bar.

"Thanks."

She nodded. "I can tell when someone has been fucked," she said. "Or not fucked enough. Either case, don't let the bastards get you down."

I wanted to take the two bucks back.

I went outside into the sunshine. I leaned against the brick building, pulled off the top of the paper cup, then took a gulp of the drink.

It tasted good.

Warmed the cockles of my heart.

I closed my eyes.

"Everything OK?"

I opened my eyes. Tom was standing a few feet from me.

"What the fuck?" I asked. "Where did you come from?"

"I was driving by and thought I saw you go in here, so I drove in to check."

I laughed. "No. Tucson is that small?"

He shrugged. "What can I say? I was looking for a place to get a burger and a beer. Is this a good place?"

"I have no idea," I said. "I got some orange juice." I held the cup out to him. "Sprinkled with vodka."

Tom came to stand under the overhang next to me and leaned against the wall.

"Day not going well?" he asked.

"I still can't get a hold of Jake," I said. "And we still don't know if the school shooter is on his way down here to exact some kind of revenge. And now Jake's brother tells me Jake is drinking again."

"That's not good," Tom said.

"No shit," I said.

"And you didn't know?" he asked.

"I still don't know," I said. "His brother is full of so much shit. And he's a drama king, stirring up trouble or trying to. I think he and Jules are in cahoots to make me miserable and blame me for everything wrong in our lives. He said Jake hid it from me because Jake was afraid I'd leave him and run off with you." I took another gulp of vodka juice. It tasted so good. Maybe this was why people drank: It be good.

"Is that a possibility?" Tom asked.

"That I would leave Jake because he was drinking or run off with you?"

"Either. Both."

I sighed. "You remember what it was like," I said.

Tom shook his head. "No. You hardly talked about it."

"Which was fine with you."

"Which was fine with me. I guess."

"Jake is such a good man," I said. "I loved him so much. Love him so much. And the real him disappeared. He reminded me of my mother. She just went away. And my father who was a drunk most of my childhood. Where was the man I loved? Jake wouldn't get help. Wouldn't stop drinking. I couldn't watch it any more. So I told him all that. I wasn't deserting him. I wasn't giving up on him. I couldn't do anything to help. I didn't want his kids watching him disappear. Couldn't do it."

After I left Jake, Tom had work in the Portland area for a few months, so I stayed with him part of the week when Jake came and stayed with the kids. Jake rented an apartment in Vancouver. He started going to a therapist and AA. Our whole family went to a therapist. Jake worked hard to stop drinking. Instead of taking a drink when he had a panic attack, he called his sponsor. Or started telling me more often. And then we would hold each other again, wrapping our arms and legs around each other until it was OK. Or at least bearable.

We slowly put our family back together.

It probably helped that Tom returned to Michigan to his family.

"I bet this will all blow over soon," Tom said.

"I can feel this vodka," I said. "Wow. It really takes the edge off."

Tom laughed. "Been a long time since you drank, eh? Not even during the worst parts of the pandemic?"

"No!" I said. "I couldn't get drunk when my husband is an alcoholic."

I pulled out my phone and looked at it. No messages from anyone.

"Do you want to go back to your hotel and have sex?" I asked.

Tom looked at me. "Not if you're drunk."

"I'm not drunk."

"Then, yes, I would like that."

"Good." I nodded and sipped my drink.

After a few moments, Tom said, "So are we going?"

"Naw. I needed to know. A woman ain't worth anything in this culture unless some man wants to fuck her. So I guess I know I've still got some value."

He gave me a look; I shrugged. "Glad I could be of service," he said. "If we're not going to have sex, you wanna get a burger and a beer here?"

"I can't," I said. "I've gotta go to my daughter's baseball game. My daughter who hates me."

"Your daughter is playing baseball?"

"Shut up. You know she's playing softball, but it's still fucking baseball as far as I'm concerned with a bigger slower ball."

Tom folded his arms across his chest and stared at me.

"I'm sick of it all," I said. "There is a constant diminishment of girls and women, and I'm fucking tired of it. Don't you ever think about that, with your daughter?"

He shrugged. "I'm glad every day that she's OK."

"That's what I mean," I said. "Our culture is awash in violence. Small white boys with guns and very small penises."

"What? There's a correlation between school shooters and small dicks?"

"Must be," I said. "I know there's a correlation between men with those giant trucks and small dicks."

"It ain't the meat, it's the motion."

"Said some guy with a very tiny dick," I said. "Although I had a boyfriend in college with a huge dick."

"Do I really need to hear this?"

"He was so proud of it," I said. "It was awful. Scared the shit out of me. It was too big for my veejay, that's for sure."

Tom chuckled. "So what you're saying is the Goldilocks version of penises is what will keep everything OK."

I sipped loudly on my drink and then looked up at Tom. "What I'm saying is that we don't need less guns so much as we need less penises."

"I have no response to that," Tom said. "I'm gonna get something to eat and drink. You sure you're not drunk? OK to drive?"

"I'm fine." I didn't feel drunk or tipsy. I felt a little less anxious.

"I'm sure Jake is all right," Tom said.

"Yes," I said. "Jake better be all right. If he's not, I will beat the shit out of him. Metaphorically speaking, of course."

Chapter Eight

Tom went into Lucy's, and I went to my car. What was wrong with me? I had held it together for so long. Too long? I had taken care of everything and everyone. Right? Hadn't I?

I rested my head on the steering wheel. Jake was all right. He was OK. He had just lost track of time. Or he lost his phone. We couldn't have another terrible thing happen. I mean, we could. It happened to people all the time.

I felt like I was going to throw up. Perhaps I should have eaten something before drinking a screwdriver in the middle of the day.

Maybe I was a little drunk.

I couldn't drive.

Could I?

If I did drive, how could I ever argue that I wasn't like all the other assholes who did whatever they wanted, thinking only of themselves?

"Fuck me."

I got a text. Please be Jake. Please be Jake.

It was from Jules. She wanted to stay at Daisy's tonight.

"Go for it," I answered her.

I texted Tom. "Shouldn't drive. Can you give me a ride to the game?"

No answer. I watched the door to Lucy's. A few minutes later, the door opened. Tom came out carrying a white take-out bag and a paper cup. I got out of my car, locked it, and walked to Tom's SUV. He handed me the bag when I got to him. I took it and went to the passenger's door, opened it, and got in. Tom put the cup in the holder by the gear shift as he got into the SUV.

"It's pop," he said. "No liquor. And I got you a fish sandwich and fries. They'll soak up the liquor. Tell me how to get there from here."

"Thanks, Tom."

I had to get directions to the field from my phone. I didn't know much about where anything was in this town. I usually drove south to get away from the city. I instructed Tom while I ate the fish sandwich and fries. I couldn't believe the amount of junk food I had eaten today.

Twenty minutes later, we were at the field. I looked around for Jake's truck. I didn't see it. Tom and I sat in his SUV together, eating. The car smelled of grease.

"What if Jake is really gone?" I said. "What if he's run off? He apparently does have an extra ten thousand dollars."

"What?"

"Oh yeah," I said. "I was keeping that to myself. Jake's boss thinks he stole ten thousand dollars. He was supposed to put it in the bank and it never made it there."

"That doesn't sound good," Tom said. "It also doesn't sound like Jake."

"How would you know? You've only met him a few times."

"And you've been describing him to me for twenty years,"

Tom said. "He sounded like a saint. So unless you were bullshitting me, I don't think he'd steal ten thousand dollars."

"Unless his alcohol problem morphed into a gambling addiction," I said. "I've heard of that happening. And maybe he owed someone money." I hung my head. "I'm completely baffled. I hope he shows up here! I want to hear all the logical explanations for everything that has happened today."

Tom grabbed the bag and wrappings and threw everything in the trash behind his seat. He opened the window. Fresh air wafted in. I could hear people in the stands talking. Heard the sound of a ball hitting leather as the teams practiced.

"Are you looking forward to the game?" Tom asked.

I glanced over at him. "Are you making small talk?"

"I'm trying to," he said. "I'm kind of at a loss here."

"No, I hate going to these things," I said. "The truth is that I'm bored at them. I'd rather be out there playing. Or whatever they're doing. I don't like being in the audience. I felt that way at the library after a while. Like I was just directing people. I wasn't really part of anything. I liked spending time with Jake and the kids at the games. That was nice. But I was also waiting for it to end. For something bad to happen. I like being outside on a trail, watching for birds or other wild things. And I like writing. I like making up stories. Writing about other people."

"But aren't you on the sidelines then?" he asked.

"No!" I said. "I am the creator. I have control over life and death. It's comforting to write about other people's traumas. Maybe because they're not real. Or maybe because I can make it all right for the good people and ruin the bad people."

Tom laughed.

"You don't see people as good or bad, do you?" I said.

Tom shrugged. "Most people are trying to get through the day as best they can."

"Jake is the same way," I said. "Not me. I want the bad people punished. I want good people to thrive. That's the way the world should work."

"But it doesn't," Tom said.

"No, it doesn't," I said. "And because I birthed children, I guess I have to go watch this game. Thanks for bringing me. You've been a doll. You have been good to me."

"Except when I wasn't."

I looked at him. "You know, we didn't get along because we want different things. I wanted someone who adored me above all else. I needed that. I wanted someone to catch me whenever I fell."

"I would have done that," he said. "Or at least I would have tried."

"Half the time you wouldn't have even noticed I fell," I said. "Or that I needed anything at all."

"Because you didn't need anything," he said. "You took care of yourself. You told me that. You told me that was one of the things you loved about Jake. He never treated you like you were less than because you were a woman. I never did that either."

"I know," I said. I didn't really know, but I didn't want to argue with him. It was too difficult to explain. Tom was fun to fuck, but we ultimately came from two different worlds. In his world, the women sat around talking and cooking and taking care of children while the guys stood around grilling steaks, drinking beer, and talking sports. At night the men and the women occasionally had mediocre sex.

That was my view of his world. I didn't ask him what his view of my world was.

I was suddenly so tired.

"I better go," I said. "I enjoy your visits. It is less exhausting to be around you than it is to be around so many other people. Usually. Today is stressful."

"If you need me later, come on over," he said. "Or text. My hotel is three blocks away."

I nodded. I got out of the SUV, closed the door, and walked toward the bleachers. I looked back at Tom and waved. He nodded. Then I looked around for Mattie. He was in the part of the stands that were in the shade. Weren't a lot of spectators. I was glad. I wasn't comfortable in crowds. Less people, less guns, I figured.

Mattie waved. Sitting next to him were Jake's parents. I hurried up the bleachers to them. I kissed them both on the cheek.

"They're about to start," Mattie said.

"Have you heard from Jake?" I asked as I sat in front of Mattie.

"He stopped by the house this morning," Jake's mother Izzy said. "I was at the store, I guess. Santi told me later."

Santiago was watching the field. "Where is Jules?"

"She's in the outfield," Mattie said.

"Oh, there she is." Santiago stood and waved. "Juliet!" he called. Jules waved.

"Before he showed the house in Vail?" I asked. Couldn't have been. He was having breakfast with me.

"I dunno," Santiago said. "He didn't mention."

"Why was he there?" I asked.

"I dunno." Santiago.

I was starting to get annoyed with him.

"Mom, I'm gonna go sit with Jimmy for a while," Mattie said. I nodded.

When he was out of earshot, I said, "Pedro came over to the house. He said Jake has been drinking. Do you know anything about that?"

"No!" Izzy said. "Couldn't be."

Santiago didn't say anything.

"He has been by the house a lot," Izzy said. "Anything going on at home?"

"No," I said.

"He comes over several times a week," Izzy said.

"He does stop by the bar," Santiago said. "I've seen his car there. I dunno if he drinks. I don't go in."

Izzy glanced at him.

"What about that Josie Martinez?" Izzy asked. "Is she there when he's there?"

"I told you I dunno. I don't go in. No more. No mas."

"Who is Josie Martinez?" I asked.

"Jake never told you about her?" Izzy asked. She put up her hand. "Not up to me to tell. When they were in high school, she was around. If they had a relationship or not, I don't know. But she wanted to marry Jake. Claimed her baby was his at first, but then she backed down. Admitted she was lying. Then when he moved back here, when you all moved back, she started going after him again."

I blinked. So much for Izzy not saying anything.

This sounded like straight up gossip to me. It was one of the reasons I didn't like being around family. Too much gossip. Too much of this drama. I didn't want drama or trauma.

Jake wouldn't cheat on me. And he wouldn't have anything to do with someone like this Josie Martinez. Claiming he fathered a baby when he was in high school. Bullshit. Izzy must be remembering that wrong. Jake would have told me.

"She lives a couple of blocks from us. That small dark blue house with the white trim on the corner of Pennsylvania and 4th. You remember it."

I did remember it. The blue was so dark it almost looked black.

"Not that Jake would have anything to do with her normally," Izzy said. "But when the Acosta men drink, they get a little handsy."

The crowd cheered. I had no idea why. I glanced over at Mattie. He and Jimmy were looking down at their phones. Out in the field, Jules was watching the batter.

"You mean Santiago and Pedro?" I asked. Because Jake did not drink when he was young.

"No, not Santiago. Pedro, maybe. Jake, too."

"Izzy, what are you talking about? I've been with Jake for twenty years. He never drank until after the shooting."

"A couple years in high school," Izzy said. "He was hanging with the wrong people. Drank too much. He kissed a girl. She didn't want it. He was suspended from school."

"Jake?" I asked. She nodded.

No. Jake didn't treat girls or women like that. Like they were nothing but things for the pleasure of men. No, no, no. He wouldn't, couldn't, didn't. Not ever.

"He stopped drinking after that," Izzy said. "And then Josie said the baby was his. I think she thought if she said that, Jake would marry her because he was such a good guy."

"What happened?"

"Jake swore the baby was not his," Izzy said. "I believed him. I went and talked with Josie's parents. She finally admitted if wasn't Jake's. She went away for a while. When she came back, no baby." Izzy shrugged. "Who knows if there ever was one. But she does have a thing for Jake."

"Do you have her phone number?" I asked.

Izzy looked at me. "Why?"

"Because Jake isn't here," I said. "And he's not home. I can't find him. Maybe this Josie Martinez knows where he is. He had SH written in his calendar for today. Whatever that means."

"Jake don't have nothing to do with her," Santiago said, not looking at me. "He'll be home soon."

"Do you know something I don't?" I asked.

"No, I just know."

Izzy got out her phone. Looked for something. Did something. I heard my phone. I looked at it. Josie Martinez's number.

"Thanks. I'll be back."

I hurried down the stands and walked over to an empty picnic table under an old sycamore tree. Then I phoned Josie Martinez.

"Hello? Who are you?" A woman's voice.

"Is this Josie?" I asked.

"Yes, who the fuck are you?"

"I'm looking for Jake Acosta," I said.

"He's here," she said. "What do you want with him?" She sounded drunk.

I was relieved and horrified all at the same time.

"Can I talk to him?" I asked.

"He's taking a piss," she said. "What do you want? Are you that bitch of a wife? How'd you find him?"

"Isabella Acosta gave me your number."

"That bitch," the woman said. "She's trying to keep me from her boys. Like I'm gonna contaminate them."

"Can I talk to him?" I asked. "I want to know if he's OK."

"He is fine," she said. "You know, he is still hard as a rock. Can go all night long. Can't do that with you, can he?" She giggled. "I let him drink. I let him eat. Me. He can eat me. I let him fuck. And fuck. And fuck."

"Tell me where you are," I said, "so I can come get him."

"Come get him?" She laughed and then coughed. "Don't you get it? He doesn't want to see you. He is never coming back."

"Please, tell him he needs to call his kids. They're worried."

"Fuck off," she said.

And the call was over.

What just happened? Jesus H. Christ.

What just happened?

The world was throbbing.

Thank god he was OK.

But what the fuck?

I called her number again. It rang twice and then hung up. I tried several more times.

I sat on the picnic table listening to the world throb.

I had had a life this morning. It wasn't perfect but it was good.

Now it was all gone. Again.

I hung my head.

We had gone through this before when Jake started drinking after the shooting. He would disappear. I would spend hours looking for him and then retrieve him from some bar or some friend's house.

Never a woman's home. That wasn't Jake's style.

At least, I hadn't thought so.

I wearily looked at my phone. I saw a new message from Mattie. He wanted to spend the night at Jimmy's. Fine with me. I texted both kids that I had found Dad, and he'd talk to them later. I added, "I'm not feeling well. I'm leaving the game early."

Then I started walking. Maybe running. I could barely see or think. Somehow I got to Tom's hotel. Motel. Whatever it was called. I went to the door and knocked on it. It opened almost immediately.

"Christ, what happened?" Tom asked.

Chapter Nine

Tom closed the door behind me as I sat on his bed.

"I'm sorry," I said.

He dragged the chair in the corner forward a bit and then sat in it so he was closer to me.

"I found Jake," I said. "He's at some woman's house he used to date in high school. Or something. I wasn't really clear on it. She said some nasty things to me. Sounds like Jake has been spilling his guts to her about our sex life."

Tom frowned.

"I'm so angry right now," I said, "and completely defeated. I feel like it's starting all over again. Except before I lived in a place where I had friends. I knew where to go and what to do. Here, I don't have anything or anyone."

"Did you talk to him?" Tom asked.

"No. When I called, she wouldn't let me."

"He'll probably sober up and come home in the morning," Jake said. "Isn't that what used to happen?"

"Sometimes," I said. "But often I went and got him. Until I

refused to do it. He probably doesn't know that Colin Moore escaped, and he needs to know. If Colin is on his way to Tucson, he could be here tonight."

"Maybe you and the kids should get a hotel for the night," Tom said.

"The kids are staying at friends," I said.

"You can stay here then," he said.

"That's kind," I said, "but I want to go to Patagonia and get Jake."

"Oh man," he said. "Are you sure?"

"No," I said. "But I don't know who this woman is. She sounds like a crazy drunken asshole."

"Wait until the morning," he said. "Everyone should be sober by then."

"And how many more times will they have fucked by the morning?" I said.

"Does it matter?" Tom asked.

I bit my lip. "What if she's lying?" I said. "Jake's mom said she had a thing for Jake, so maybe she was lying to me. Maybe nothing has happened yet."

Tom shrugged. "Hey, it's your marriage."

"This is nothing like our marriage," I said. "Will you come with me? I might still be a little tipsy and the roads are windy on the way to Patagonia. And it's getting dark."

Tom stood. "Let's go."

"Thanks."

"What are fuck friends for?" he asked.

"I don't think we're that any longer," I said. "Friends, but not fuck friends."

"We'll see," he said as he opened the door. "The night is young."

I laughed in spite of myself.

We got into Jake's car and drove out of town. I wanted to be the one driving. I hated sitting in the passenger's seat. We headed south on a two lane highway.

"If you go the speed limit," I said, "they'll ride your ass. Go five miles above and they'll leave you alone. Took me a while to learn that. But go the speed limit on the curves. They're dangerous."

Tom glanced over at me but didn't say anything.

"Sorry," I said. "Being a backseat driver." I sighed. "I've got so many questions. Like what happened to trigger his drinking? Pedro says he's been drinking since we moved here. Jesus. I hope that's not true."

"Addicts gotta addict," Tom said. "You told me that."

"I completely forgot that today is the anniversary of the shooting," I said. "We've been arguing."

"I didn't know you guys argued," Tom said.

We were away from the city and the sprawl now. Some of the mesquite tree-dotted landscape still had the pink of sundown on it.

"He says I can't understand some things about his life. And that's true. I don't know what it's like to be Mexican-American, and he doesn't understand what it's like to be a woman."

"That's what you argue about?" Tom asked. "I think that would drive me to drink, too."

"Shut up," I said. "It's—it's that I'm tired. The world feels so fucked up. All these messes, and I'm supposed to clean them up, and I had nothing to do with them."

"Messes?"

I made a noise. "You wouldn't understand. And it feels so much worse since the shooting and then the pandemic and the insurrection. Christ on a crutch. Jake wants me to find some joy."

"What a prick."

"He wants me to find joy, and then he goes missing, steals

ten thousand dollars, and fucks some skank in Patagonia. He's not helping."

"For someone who doesn't like drama in her life, it sounds like a lot of drama."

"Why did you come to Arizona now, really? Obviously I was wrong about you traveling here for work."

"You really want to know?" he asked.

"Yes," I said.

"I wanted to see how you and Jake were doing. If you weren't doing well, I was hoping you'd come back to Michigan with me. Or I'd stay here in Arizona with you."

I laughed. "You are joking, right?"

"Well, that depends."

"Jesus, Tom. You can't be serious. We would kill each other."

He shrugged. "You asked."

We drove in silence for a few minutes. Then I said, "You come to me on my daughter's wedding day and ask me this favor?"

Tom grimaced. "Yeah, well."

"Do you remember when we went to see The Godfather?" I asked.

"I think we were the only ones in the theater," he said.

"We were up in a balcony or something," I said. "Some theater in Ann Arbor that played classics."

"Yep. The Michigan?"

"I don't think so," I said. "Do you remember we were fooling around?"

He laughed. "Yes. We were fooling around. Couldn't keep our hands off one another."

"I went down on you there," I said. "Do you remember? One of the very few times."

"Yes, I remember."

I glanced over at him. He was smiling.

"I don't understand why men like that so much."

He shrugged. "It feels nice."

"Maybe to you," I said. "To me I've got this big thing in my mouth that has urine or cum on it. Or did."

"Ewww," he said. "I never thought about it that way. I never forced you."

"Every time we made out, you pushed my head down. You wanted it."

"We hadn't figured out actual intercourse yet," he said. "I pushed your head down? I don't remember that at all. I may have guided your head, you know, in the dark."

"No, that's not how it was," I said.

"I didn't realize," he said.

"Me trying to pull my head away wasn't a clue?" I asked.

"I-I guess not," he said. "Why didn't you ever say anything?"

"I did. But you know, I was a teenage girl. I wanted to please my guy."

"I'm sorry," he said.

I shrugged. "You were a teenage boy. Your daddy didn't teach you better. Jake and I have had extensive talks with Mattie about his responsibilities as a man. Just because he wants a blow job doesn't mean some girl—or guy, if he chooses—has to give him one. He is mortified when we talk about these things, but we talk about them anyway."

"Is that why we broke up?" Tom asked.

"When?" I asked. "Which time? You broke up with me several times and broke my heart, and I broke up with you. I don't remember when it became permanent. I remember soon after graduation we went to a party. We were broken up, but I really wanted to be with you. I didn't understand why we weren't together. And I got really drunk. We went out in the woods together. I don't remember why. Maybe we were gonna make out. It was disgusting how much I wanted to get back with you. But once we were out there in the woods, I got really sick and dizzy from drinking. Do you remember this?"

Tom didn't say anything.

"So you picked me up and threw me over your shoulder," I said. "But that made me even sicker. I begged you to put me down. Finally you threw me to the ground, and you started yelling at me and kicking me. I was so sick I could hardly move, but you kept kicking me and yelling at me. And then you went away. You left me in the woods on the ground. I couldn't move. I remember breathing in the woods and listening to the crickets and wondering when someone was gonna come murder me. Because our classmate Patty had been murdered by then. So many women and girls had been murdered by then. Do you remember?"

"I was drunk, too."

"My friends found me and brought me home," I said. "In the morning, I had bruises all over my body. And I called you and apologized. I called you and fucking apologized. Jesus."

Tom sighed.

"We never really came back from that, Tom, from me humiliating myself by apologizing to you and you fucking accepting my apology."

"We were kids."

"You're looking back and trying to remember all the times you forced your wife to do something sexual she didn't want to do, aren't you?"

"A little bit," he said. "Although I can't remember her being in a lot of my memories. It's the pleasure I remember."

I snorted. "And there it is."

"Couldn't you have told me this years ago?"

"I suppose I could have," I said. "But I assumed you figured it out because I haven't sucked your cock since we were teens. But it's not only that. It's all the things men think they have a right to and a right to do, and they don't think about it. And women don't want to talk about it either. I've tried having conversations about male power with other women and I swear most of the time, they feel sorry for the men! Who hates women more than men? Other women."

"I don't hate women," Tom said.

"Sure you don't," I said. "As long as we're pleasing you. Every boy or man I ever dated loved my energy, loved my spirit, and then they wanted to fucking crush it. Crush me. Tame it. Tame me. Change me. Including you. Jake was the only one. Jake has said I am a fucking force of nature. I am elemental. He has never tried to change a hair on my head. He has never tried to force me to do anything for his sexual pleasure." I felt like I was gonna scream again. I rubbed my face. "So I guess to answer your question: No, Jake and I are not doing fine. But no, I'm not gonna run off with you or anyone else. At least not right now. I've got to see if my husband has turned into an asshole like everyone else or not."

"I guess you're lucky you two are together," Tom said.

"Luck had nothing to do with it," I said. "I picked him. I saw all these girls and women picking assholes—and I remembered choosing assholes myself over the years—so this time I decided to pick a good man."

"I guess the implication is I was not a good man?"

I shrugged. "You weren't my good man. And maybe Jake wasn't either. Maybe I expected too much from him. Of him. I'm so tired of everything being so chaotic. I want a normal fucking life."

Tom laughed. "Come on. You never wanted a normal life. You never wanted the picket fence or any of that."

"I wanted adventure," I said. "Not this bullshit. What man

would put up with this crap? Looking for their spouse in a bar or out with someone else?"

"From what you've told me, Jake would," Tom said. "I would. I'd look for you."

I shook my head. "Now you're sticking up for him?"

"Just the facts, ma'am."

We drove in silence for a long while. I supposed I should have waited to spill my guts until after we got to Patagonia. Or after I got home. I didn't care. It had been a long day. I was grateful to Tom. If I found Jake in bed with another woman, maybe I would take Tom back to his motel and fuck his brains out. Because that was the way the world . . . didn't worked.

I had this overwhelming urge to apologize to Tom. Apologize for speaking up. For telling him all of this as he was doing me a favor. I was alone with him in a car at night, a long way from home. I glanced over at him. What if I had made him angry? I shook my head. No. He would never hurt me, not again. He had been a boy all those years ago when he kicked me, when he left me in the woods in the dark. He had been a drunk kid. We had all done stupid dangerous things when we were young.

I hoped no one ever beat the shit out of my daughter and left her alone and vulnerable, unable to move, in the dark, in the woods. Or my son, for that matter, but I knew he had less to worry about than my daughter. That was the truth.

"Did you ever hit a woman again?" I asked. "After that night when you dropped me to the forest floor and then kicked me over and over."

"No," he said. "I've never hit a woman before or after that. Never hit a man either. That was a period of time when life was very confusing and frustrating. I know that sounds like an excuse. I can't even imagine it now."

"Bet you're glad you came to Arizona to declare your love for me now, aren't you?"

Tom laughed and shook his head.

"Don't you ever feel like it's all wrong?" I asked. "But you can't figure out how to fix it. Like we're all under some kind of cultural spell that keeps us doing the same stupid things over and over."

"It all works for me, pretty much," Tom said.

I made a noise. "Of course it does. You old white man! Except you're divorced a couple of times. You feel like shit. And you have trouble developing deep sustaining relationships."

"Pretty much like everyone else," he said. "That's life."

"That's my point," I said. "People accept the unacceptable. Why? We have children being gunned down in their schools. How is that acceptable?"

"It isn't," Tom said.

"But it's happening almost every day," I said. "And remember that it didn't used to be that way. And it's not that way in other places. We accept the unacceptable."

"What's the answer?"

"I have no fucking idea," I said. "An end to the patriarchy. Connection with nature. Clearly I have no answers since I'm in a car with you driving to a small border town to try and find my drunk philandering husband."

"I don't think about things like this," he said. "I don't think I've ever thought about these things or had a conversation with anyone about any of them."

"I guess in your world you don't have to, eh? I mean, fuck, Tom, the skies were so dark in Michigan last summer from wildfires in Canada that you couldn't go outside."

"I went outside."

"You shouldn't have been outside," I said. "Air pollution should not be the norm. Half the world should not be covered in smoke from wildfires caused by climate change. How do you not think of these things?"

He turned on the radio. Purple Rain came on. "I notice they play a lot of Prince here," Tom said. "In Portland, I remember they played a lot of Led Zeppelin. In Detroit, it's Bob ."

I shook my head and held up my hands, thumbs up.

And then somehow time passed, and we were coming into the small town of Patagonia. I had rarely been here at night, and it was nearly as dark as being out in the desert or forest at night.

"Turn here," I said. We went down 4th Street for a block or two. There was Pennsylvania Avenue. And the dark blue house that looked black in the night. Her front porch light was on.

"I guess she doesn't give a shit about the birds," I said.

"What?" Tom asked.

"Stop here."

He stopped. I felt like a ball of adrenaline. Right now, I wanted to see Jake and know he was OK. Then I could punch him in the face.

As I ran across the street toward the house, I looked around for Jake's truck. Didn't see it. Had he already left?

I ran up the steps and pounded on the door. I could hear a woman's and a man's voice inside. Didn't recognize either. I pounded again and pushed on the doorbell. Heard footsteps.

I rang the doorbell again. "Shut up!" I recognized that scream from the phone.

The door swung open.

And Pedro was standing in the doorway, light from the house turning him almost completely black.

"Where's Jake?" I asked.

The woman came to stand next to Pedro. She was half-dressed, although I couldn't tell which half. She was fucking gorgeous despite her smeared mascara and smeared red mouth. Her black hair covered half her face.

"What are you doing here?" Pedro asked.

"The same reason you're here," I said. "To get Jake."

"Who is this slut?" the woman asked. "Is this your wife? Is this the bitch I talked to earlier? I told you to get lost." She was slurring her words, and her eyes were half-closed.

"Go inside," Pedro said. He pushed the woman too hard back into the house.

"You told me Jake was here," I said. "Just an hour ago. I want to take him home. You said they were fucking each other's brains out!"

"Jake?" The woman came back out and leaned on Pedro. He put his arm around her waist to hold her up.

"Why would Jake be here?" she said. "Oh, your mother." She giggled. "I didn't know you were looking for Jake Acosta. Jake isn't here. I don't fuck brothers. Not if they're related to each other."

"Go back inside," Pedro said. He had an edge to his voice. He came toward me. I backed down off the porch.

"I thought you were looking for Jake," I said. "What's going on? Is that Josie Martinez? Your mom told me she was after Jake, and then Josie told me Jake was here."

Pedro shook his head. "No. Jake isn't here! My mom thinks every woman is after Jake."

"So you and Josie are having an affair?" I asked. "What's your wife think of that?"

"My wife doesn't know," Pedro said.

"You are two blocks from your parents' house!" I said. "How could she not know?" Who cared? I put my hand up. "I don't care. Where is Jake?"

"I don't know," Pedro said. "He's been my smokescreen for a while. My mom will see me with Josie, and I'll tell her Josie was looking for Jake. Stupid. We've been doing this since high school."

"You said Jake was drinking," I said. "You came to the house to tell me that!"

"That was all true," he said. "He's been at bars with me. I dunno if he was drinking. Tonight I've been to all the bars I know that he knows about. I didn't find him."

"Pedro, she is drunk out of her mind," I said. "She told me Jake was with her. She said things that only Jake could have told her." Unless Pedro was having some of the same problems Jake had had.

Pedro shook his head. "Jake is not here. He's never been here."

"I need to see for myself," I said.

"She's not going to like that," Pedro said.

"I don't give a fuck," I said. "Keep her away from me."

I ran up the steps again. I could feel Pedro behind me.

"What's going on?" Josie slurred. She reached for me, lost her balance, and fell on her butt on the couch. I hurried through the tiny house: living room, kitchen, bathroom, bedroom. It all smelled like alcohol and nightmares. I wanted to throw up. I opened every closed door. Looked under the bed.

"I wouldn't be hiding my own brother," Pedro said.

I was out the door again before Josie could get off her ass. Pedro followed me.

"What are you doing here?" I asked. "Please tell me you are not fucking her. She's so drunk she can barely stand."

"I-I just stopped by," he said. "Don't tell my parents. Please. Jake knows, but not my parents or wife. Not my kids."

"Jesus, Pedro," I said. "This is too icky for words. I thought you were looking for your brother. Instead—." I looked at him. "You smell like drunk."

If Jake wasn't here, where was he? Maybe he had shown up at the game. Or maybe he was home.

I ran across the street and got into the SUV.

"Where is Jake?" Tom asked.

"I have no idea."

Chapter Ten

I asked Tom to drive slowly around town so we could look for Jake's truck, just in case. We drove by his parents' house, but it was dark. They might still be at the game.

Then we headed back to Tucson. I had a knot in my stomach the size of Jupiter. I was so terrified I could barely breathe.

"Tom, where is Jake?" I whispered.

"I don't know, darlin'," Tom said, "but I'm sure he's fine."

I texted both of the kids to see how they were doing. I didn't mention Jake. Both of them responded. Jules didn't say anything snarky. She didn't say whether they had won or lost the game. Then I checked the news. Colin Moore was still on the run. The police still didn't know where he was. I texted Stephanie to see if she knew anything else. She didn't.

Tom and I barely spoke to one another on the way back. I wanted to get home and find Jake there. How could I have believed Jake was with that woman? Jesus. Or even that he was drinking again. It was possible that the anniversary of the shooting had affected me in ways I didn't realize. I didn't trust anything or anyone again.

We stopped at the border checkpoint on the way back. As we drove up to it, Tom whispered to me, "This is 50 miles from the border. What's it all about?"

I shrugged. "Power and humiliation."

They waved us through with barely a glance.

"Every time Jake visits his parents or they visit us, they have to go through that fucking checkpoint. He is constantly hassled. Has to prove he's an American."

"How does he do that?" Tom asked as we sped away.

"Answers their stupid questions and shows them his driver's license," I said. "Once we were coming out here, and Border Patrol pulled us over. It was when the pandemic was still pretty bad. I wouldn't roll down the window until the guy put on a mask. He was so angry. He was cursing and yelling at us. I asked him why they had pulled us over. He said our car was dusty, and he saw a handprint on the trunk. He thought we were smuggling someone in our trunk. I said 'we live in the fucking desert. It's dusty.' I popped the trunk, and he looked inside and they let us go. Jake was quiet through the whole thing. When we were far away, he said, 'They could have killed us and they would have gotten away with it. They'd have some excuse for why they did it.'"

"He'd know," Tom said. "This is where he's from."

"Yeah," I said. "I should have kept my mouth shut."

At the time, I was angry. It hadn't occurred to me then that the rising tensions and the underlying beat of violence might have reminded Jake of the shooting. Both the border guards had weapons. One was Anglo, the other was Latino. The brown man was the one who was angry at me. The white guy stood back a bit and watched. No one was hurt that day, but I felt in danger the entire time.

When we got to town, I had Tom take me to my car at Lucy's parking lot.

"Do you want me to follow you home?" Tom asked.

"No," I said. "I'm OK. I'll talk to you tomorrow. I really appreciate everything you did today."

I got out of the SUV, went to my car, and headed home. When I got there, I saw that Jake's truck was still gone. I had gotten no messages from him.

I went into the house. My body throbbed with fear and tension. I texted Stephanie. "Any sign of CM?"

She immediately wrote back. "No."

It had been nearly twelve hours since I had last heard from Jake. That was unprecedented.

I went to the computer and looked up our bank accounts. Nothing had been added or subtracted in the last couple of days. Then I went to our credit cards. We only had two, and one we only used in emergencies. One of the credit cards had been used around 1:00 p.m. in Sonoita. For ten dollars—because the gas was so expensive there. He must have been running low and wanted enough to get him home with a cushion. 1:00 p.m. That wasn't so long ago. He must be OK. Maybe he went to see old friends. But he would have gotten a hold of me whether he had his phone or not.

Or he stopped at a bar and he had gotten drunk. Then it's possible he wouldn't have called.

In any case, something was very wrong.

I called the police and put in a missing person report. Turned out all those TV shows were wrong: I didn't have to wait 48 hours. They asked me all kinds of questions: Did he have any medical conditions? Was he a danger to himself or anyone else? Where was he going when he went missing?

I told them about the shooting and this being the anniversary of the shooting. I said he normally kept in touch. I gave them his work phone and his home phone. I told them everything I could think of telling them—except about the missing ten thousand dollars. Nope. I knew he didn't steal that money, and I wasn't going to risk putting Jake in some kind of danger with the police. I didn't tell them he was an alcoholic either. But I told them everything else.

I was on the phone for a long time. I kept listening for Jake's truck. For his footsteps. The terror grew. When I got off the phone with the police, I called all the hospitals and open clinics in the county. Asking if a Jake Acosta was there or if there was anyone matching his description. Then I remembered his birth name was Santiago Acosta, Jr. So I had to call several places back and ask again with the right name.

I was so exhausted I couldn't even cry. I sat on the couch shaking. I couldn't call anyone to ask for advice. Or to tell me it would be all right. I had learned that after the shooting. It was my fault, I supposed. I had left home, moved away, and wasn't in that much contact with my family for years. And then Mom died. And then Dad. I barely knew my sisters. Tom was the only one from high school I knew.

Why hadn't I made friends anywhere else?

Was not going to go down that road now.

I pulled my legs up and put my chin on my knees. I reached over and switched off the light. Now I was in the dark. Nothing else to do. Nothing I could do. Except wait.

I called Jake's parents and told them Jake was officially missing. I asked them to let his siblings know, in case he got in touch with one of them. His mother said, "Don't worry. He'll be back before you know it." I thought, well, I know it, and he's not back. I vaguely wondered why she wasn't more upset. If my kid was missing, I would be going crazy. Just like I was with my husband missing.

Somehow I fell asleep on the couch. I awakened at 2 a.m. when I heard the front door open.

I jumped up, "Jake?"

"It's me, Mom." Jules' voice. A moment later I saw her. She dropped her backpack on the table.

"Is everything OK?" I asked.

"No," she said. "Dad still isn't answering me, and now his voicemail is full. I can't even leave a message. I thought you said he was OK."

She sat in the chair across from the couch.

"I thought I knew where he was," I said. "But I was wrong. Your Uncle Pedro said he thought Jake was drinking. I went looking for him. Didn't find him. I've checked the hospitals and urgent care. No Dad. I've filed a missing person report."

Her eyes widened. "Where is he? Did you guys fight or something?"

I was too tired to pretend to be patient. No matter what happened, according to Jules, it was my fault.

"No, we did not fight," I said. "When do you ever see us fight?"

She shrugged. "I don't know what happens when we're not around."

"We have a lot of sex," I said. Knowing it would gross her out.

"Ewwww," Jules said.

Yeah, well, don't fuck with me, child.

"We had breakfast after he dropped you and Mattie off," I said. "Then he left to meet a client in Vail. Did he say anything to you and Mattie on the way to school? Everything seem OK?"

She ran her fingers through her hair. "He was in a good mood. We sang 'Mutiny.' We hadn't done that in a while. He kept singing the line 'let the motherfucker burn,' at the top of his lungs. He sounded so happy."

Crap.

"That is dark," I said.

"It didn't seem that way," Jules said. "It was a song. He was happy. He was Old Dad."

"What?"

"That's what Mattie and I call him," she said. "Old Dad and New Dad."

I waited.

"Old Dad was before the shooting," she said. "Before the drinking and depression. New Dad is now."

"What about when he was drinking and depressed," I said. "What did you call him then?"

"Dad," she said.

Ouch.

Was there an Old Mom and a New Mom? I wasn't gonna ask.

"I don't think he's drinking," Jules said. "He's not like he was before."

"It's late," I said. "You've got school. You better get some sleep."

"Mom," she said.

"I don't want you to worry about this," I said.

"He's my father," she said, "and he's missing. Of course I'm going to worry. He could be dead somewhere."

I flinched.

"Sorry," Jules said. "I'm just saying. I want to help."

"I have no idea what to do," I said.

"Maybe he was upset about you having lunch with Tom," she said.

"He didn't care I was having lunch with Tom."

"Did you have sex with him?"

I sighed and shook my head slightly. "Your dad was going to talk to you about this, but I guess I will. Whether I had sex with

Tom or anyone else is none of your business. It is my life, and since I'm married to your father and we have pledged to be faithful to one another, it is his business. I'd appreciate it if you would stop making cracks about my relationship with Tom. I have never been unfaithful to your father. Nothing I did caused your father to start drinking to excess."

"But you ran off with Tom," she said. "You two were hot for one another."

"Jesus, Jules," I said. "You're old enough not to be so stupid." I shouldn't have said the word stupid, but it slipped out. "Your father and I separated when he couldn't get his drinking under control. During that time, Tom and I had a relationship. Not before Dad started drinking: after. I didn't do anything wrong. I was trying to protect you and Mattie by separating from you father."

"You didn't stick by him when he needed you," Jules said. "That's what you should have done."

"He wouldn't get help," I said. "He was putting us all in danger because he wouldn't get help."

"Bullshit," she said. "He needed you and you kicked him out."

"My first obligation is to protect my children," I said, "and I did that."

"From what?" Jules said. "Dad would never hurt us or put us in danger."

"He drove drunk with you both in the car!" And that slipped out, too. I had never meant to tell them that. Or remind them. I figured they had forgotten about it by now.

"He didn't," she said. "He never did."

I got up from the couch. I couldn't do this.

"You were so tiny when you were born," I said. "And beautiful. Just as you are now. I knew as soon as I held you in my arms that I would do anything for you. You were your own person. From the beginning. I loved that about you. I still love that about you. When you were younger, you liked me and your dad. You loved us, of course, but you liked being with us. That was such a gift. We felt we were so lucky to be your parents. Mattie's too. But somewhere along the line, you decided you didn't like me. Your dad can do no wrong. I am the bad guy. I am the evil one. Everyone says that's how teenagers are: They treat their parents like shit." I looked at Jules. "Tell me, Juliet. How did I become the bad guy? What did I ever do to you?"

She looked at me. "Nothing. Everything." She shrugged. "The world is so fucked. I can't be angry with Dad. I can't blame him for anything because he would crumble. He's so fragile. I blame Colin Moore, but I can't kill him. For one thing, I can't get to him. For another, killing him would make me just like him. So then who else? Not Mattie. He's a good kid. That leaves you, Mom. Because you can take it. Come on. You can fucking take it."

"I can't take it," I said. "At least until your dad is found, I would appreciate it if you could treat me with common courtesy. I'm going to bed."

I left the room. Didn't look back. Jules said nothing. She had no idea how much restraint I had used during that conversation. I wanted to scream at her, to tell her what an insensitive brat she was. I wanted to slap her silly. But I didn't. I had never hit my kids. Ever. I was glad I didn't.

Chapter Eleven

I think I woke up every 15 minutes. I kept checking the phone. Kept looking outside. I went to Jules' door once. She had left it open. She was curled up on top of her covers. I felt myself crumbling with affection as I watched her. I wanted to curl up behind her and tell her everything would be all right.

But I wasn't going to start lying to her now.

I finally got out of bed for good before dawn. The house felt so empty without Mattie and Jake. This place, these four acres out in the Sonoran Desert, was going to be our dream house where the kids could run free. Where we would grow food. Where we would heal and learn to live again.

Instead, I learned about all the things that could kill us or make us sick: rattlesnakes, kissing bugs, killer bees, Valley Fever, rabid right-wingers. And that didn't even count all the pointy things in the desert because everything had a thorn or someway to injure. Nothing in the desert was soft or huggable. Well, maybe the cottontail rabbits, but they were dealing with their own pandemic.

I probably wouldn't have worried about many of these things if I didn't have kids. I didn't like them going to school, but they all balked at homeschooling. I was sometimes nervous when they were running around outside.

Sometimes I saw fear in their eyes when Jake or I went somewhere on our own. They wanted to know immediately when we arrived at our destinations and when we would be home. Lately, Jules was less interested in where I was.

"Jake, where are you?"

Was he hurt? Was he drunk? Was he dead? No matter how drunk he was, he wouldn't stay out of contact for this long. He knew how much we all worried.

I closed Jules' door and went into the living room. I called the police: They hadn't heard anything. I called the hospitals and urgent care. No Jake Acosta. No Santiago Acosta. No John Doe.

I called Jimmy's parents—where Mattie was staying—and asked if they could bring him home. I texted the school that the kids wouldn't be in class today.

I took a quick shower and then made breakfast: eggs, potatoes, and steamed vegetables. Simple. It was what Jake had made me yesterday.

Mattie walked into the house as Jules came into the kitchen.

"What's going on?" he asked.

"We can't find Dad," I said. "I've called the police and they're looking for him."

"I-I thought you knew where he was," Mattie said.

"I thought I did, too," I said, "but he wasn't there. I can't find anyone who has seen him since yesterday. Did he say anything to you in the car yesterday morning?"

Mattie sat at the counter. Jules sat next to him and rubbed his back. She didn't look at me. I set breakfast in front of them.

"We sang 'Mutiny' together," he said. "He said he was going

to have a good day and he hoped we all would, too. And we kissed him goodbye."

I had heard that suicidal people often get very happy just before they kill themselves: They've made the decision, and they are relieved.

Jake wasn't suicidal. Was he? He was hardly making any money. He had few friends here. Except he grew up here. He must have friends, people I didn't know about, besides Josie Martinez.

"He wouldn't kill himself, would he?" Jules asked.

"I don't think so," I said. "Why do you ask that? Did he seem unhappy to you?"

"Just checking," she said. "No, he seemed really happy."

Ugh. They associated happiness with something bad about to happen.

"It was like the day of the shooting," Jules said. "Everything was so great that morning. And then everything changed."

"I remember that morning, too," Mattie said. "I remember it as golden."

"We had lots of other mornings like that," I said, "just so you know. You remember it better or more because of what happened after."

"Really?" Mattie asked. "You mean our brains register it differently somehow?"

"Yes," I said.

"I wonder how Dad remembers it all?" Jules asked.

"Did he tell you where he was going yesterday?" I asked.

"Home to you," Mattie said. "Did he come home?"

I nodded. "Yes, we had breakfast together."

"What did you talk about?" Mattie asked.

I glanced at Jules. "About you kids," I said. "As always. By the way, I called the school and said you were staying home today, but if you want to go, that would be fine. I don't know if there's much you can do here."

"We can help," Jules said. "Mattie and I can go through Dad's office and see if there's anything."

"OK," I said. "I'm going to call his work and find out where he was going yesterday. Then we'll figure out what to do next."

We ate our breakfasts quickly. Then the kids went out to the barn. I called his work. This time Gabby answered.

"Good morning," she said. "How are you?"

"Not good," I said. "Jake never showed up. He's been missing almost twenty-four hours."

"Oh dear!" Gabby said. "That's terrible."

"I've contacted the police," I said, "so they might be calling you. Gabby, can you tell me the address of where he went yesterday in Vail."

"Well, um," she said. And then silence.

"Gabby?" I said.

"He didn't go to Vail," she said.

"What do you mean?" I asked. "He told me he had a house to show there, and you told me he went there and then let you know he was done."

"He asked me to tell you he was in Vail if you called," Gabby said.

"What?" I said. "He asked you to lie to me?"

"No!" she said. "Although I guess that's what he did. I didn't think of it that way. He said you had an anniversary coming up and he was planning something."

"Our anniversary is in June," I said.

"Oh, well, I don't know," Gabby said. "He sounded excited. He said he'd call later."

"And did he?" I asked.

"No," she said.

"Didn't that worry you?" I asked.

"No, not really."

"Thanks, Gabby," I said.

"Let me know if you hear anything," she said.

I felt like screaming, "Why?"

I ended the call. If Jake hadn't been in Vail, where had he been? Maybe I <u>had</u> seen him at Agua Caliente Park.

I texted Jules. "I have to run to Agua Caliente Park. I'll be a few minutes. Looking for Dad."

I hurried out into the cool day. The morning sunlight was turning everything gold. A Gila woodpecker alarmed on me. I waved and hurried to the car. I felt like it was all tunnel vision on the way to the park. I hoped I would see his truck there and find him inside, asleep or hungover but OK.

Hardly anyone was here this morning. I drove by the tall palms to the parking lot.

"Jake, Jake, Jake."

The parking lot had two white SUVS. No trucks. No Jake. I stopped the car and put my head down on the steering wheel. Fuck.

Someone tapped on my window. I looked over. Tom was standing there.

I unrolled the window.

"What the fuck?" I said.

"Good morning to you, too," Tom said. "Jake get home OK?"

"No," I said. "What are you doing here?"

"I liked it," he said. "So I brought my coffee here and watched the ducks. What are you doing here?"

"Looking for Jake," I said. I opened the door and got out. We both leaned against the car as we talked. "I made a police report. Checked all the hospitals."

"I thought you had to wait until someone was missing for 48 hours," he said.

"That's on TV and in the movies, I guess," I said. "I don't know how much the police will do. I haven't figured out what I should do. I don't know this place well enough. Turns out Jake lied to me yesterday. Told me he was going to Vail, but he asked his work not to tell me he wasn't there."

"Do you know why?" Tom asked.

"I have absolutely no clue," I said. "I want him to be all right. He has to be OK for the kids. And I hope he's OK for me. I'm so afraid, and I'm angry, and I want him to be OK."

"Is there anything I can do?" Tom asked.

I shook my head. "I don't know. Is there anything you can do? Can you tell me where Jake is?"

"How would I know where Jake is?"

He sounded oddly defensive.

"I didn't think you would know," I said. "I was only talking. You asked." I sighed. "When are you going home?"

"I'm scheduled to leave Sunday," he said. "But I can stay longer if you need me to."

"Don't change your plans for us," I said. "I'm hoping this will all work out in the next couple of hours. Then we could have you over for a barbecue or something."

Tom laughed. "Now that would be odd."

I felt my phone vibrate. I pulled it out.

"I gotta take this." Tom nodded. "Stephanie. What's up?"

"It turns out Colin Moore has relatives in Oro Valley," she said. "Do you know where that is?"

"Fuck," I said. "Yes. That's essentially Tucson. I guess that means they haven't caught him. Do they have any idea where he is?"

"No, it's an older car, so they can't track it," Stephanie said.

I suddenly realized I hadn't told Stephanie that Jake was missing.

"Can you get me their address," I asked, "and what kind of car it is?"

"I'll see what I can do," she said. "In any case, I'll text you their names. I bet you'll be able to figure out where they are, using your old librarian skills."

"Stephanie, Jake is missing. He's been missing for almost 24 hours."

"What the fuck?" Stephanie said. "Jesus. Do you have any idea where he might be?"

"Not a clue," I said. "I am terrified something has happened to him."

"Maybe you should call Detective Reese," Stephanie said.

"Do it for me, please," I said. "Convince her to give me the address of Colin's relatives so I can check and see if Colin is there."

"No, let the police do that," Stephanie said. "I'll make sure Reese gets a hold of the Tucson police, or whomever."

"I made a missing person's report to the Tucson police," I said.

"I'm sure it's all coincidence," Stephanie said. "He'll turn up."

"I'm glad you're sure," I said.

"I'll let you know what Reese says," Stephanie said.

I ended the call and turned to Tom. He raised his eyebrows.

"The kid from the school shooting has relatives down here," I said, "so it's possible he's coming here. Or is already down here."

"That doesn't mean he has Jake," Tom said. "Jake disappeared before that kid could have gotten here, right?"

"Please don't say Jake disappeared," I said. No, no, no.

"OK," Tom said. "So you lost track of him before the kid could have gotten here."

I nodded. Why did we keep calling him a kid? He wasn't a

kid any more. He was over twenty. He was a man: a murderous man. I rubbed my face.

"I better get home," I said. "Maybe Jake has come back."

"Sure," Tom said.

I looked at him. "Are you OK?" I asked. "You look a little lost."

"I'm fine," he said. "I'm meeting some friends later. It's all good. Let me know how it goes."

"OK." I put my arms around him, and we embraced. Then I kissed his bearded cheek. "Thanks."

"If you decide to go looking for him again and you want company," he said, "give me a call. I promise I won't ask you to run off with me."

I smiled grimly. "OK."

He opened my car door, and I slid into the seat. He closed the door and then turned and walked away. I got a text. I looked down at my phone. It was from Jules. "We found something."

Chapter Twelve

I got home a few minutes later. Still no sign of Jake. I hurried out to Jake's office in the barn. I ran my hand across Jake's car as I passed it. I opened the door to the office. Mattie sat on the couch. Jules was at Jake's desk.

"What did you find?" I asked.

Jules held up a stack of papers. "It's a book," Jules said. "Written by Dad." She held it out to me. I took it from her and sat on the small couch next to Mattie.

The first page started about a third of the way down. The title was My Last Drink. By Santiago Jacob Acosta.

"I didn't know Dad's name was Santiago," Mattie said.

I glanced over at him. "Really?"

He shrugged. "I thought that was Grandpa's name."

"It's Dad's, too," Jules said. "Haven't you ever heard Uncle Pedro call him Saint Jacob?"

"I thought he was making fun of Dad because Dad's so straitlaced—as a rule—and Uncle Pedro isn't."

"Well, that's probably why he says it," Jules said.

"Did you read any of it?" I asked.

"A couple pages. In the beginning it's about his childhood. Then later it's about the shooting."

I was surprised he had printed it out. That probably meant he was finished with it—at least the first draft. Maybe he was waiting to give it to me. The pages looked a little tattered—curled. The manuscript had been sitting out for a while.

"I looked at the ending," Jules said. "He's still alive. That has to mean something, doesn't it?"

It meant it wasn't a manifesto on him killing himself. Probably.

"Mattie has something to show you," Jules said.

I set the manuscript on the couch next to me, and then I got up and followed Mattie out the door.

"Will you get into Dad's car?" Mattie asked. "Sit in the driver's side."

"OK." I went around to the driver's door, opened it, and got inside. I left the door open.

"Now reach your right hand down," Mattie said.

I did what he asked. At first I didn't feel anything. But then my fingers grasped something hard, thin, and smooth. I pulled it out. It was Jake's phone.

"He's always losing things in this car," Jules said. "Something about the seats, I guess, but the stuff in his right pocket often slips out. Like his phone."

I tried the phone. It was either off or dead.

"There's more," Mattie said. "Keep reaching down."

I did what he asked. My fingers found an envelope. I pulled it up and looked inside. There were several checks and a ten dollar bill along with a deposit slip: for the real estate company Jake worked for. I looked at the date. This was the missing deposit, only there was only ten dollars in cash, not ten thousand. I looked at the deposit slip more closely. The total matched what I had in my hand.

That was odd. Had there been two deposits that day? Had Stuart somehow gotten the amount wrong? Seemed unlikely he would mistake ten dollars for ten thousand. Was he trying to frame Jake for something he had done? I looked at the slip closely. Nothing had been scratched out or changed. $10 not $10,000. And the deposit wasn't in Jake's handwriting. What the hell?

I took a photo of the deposit slip, got Stuart's number from his card, and sent the photo to Stuart. I texted, "It was $10 not $10,000. Looks like your handwriting. Shall I run it to the bank for you?" Pretending to be nice. Right that minute I felt angry. What was he trying to pull?

I got out of the car, stuffed the deposit into my back pocket, and returned to Jake's office with the kids. I plugged the phone into the charger. It registered 0%.

I got a text from Stephanie. She sent me the name of Colin Moore's relatives in Oro Valley. The girlfriend's car was a very old Honda hatchback, blue. At the end of her text, Stephanie wrote, "Detective Reese said don't contact the relatives no matter what. Let the local police contact them."

"Yeah, right," I said.

I sat at Jake's desk and got on the computer. The kids sat on the couch flipping through the manuscript. I typed in the relatives' names and the name of the city. I found them immediately—but not their address. They had a studio apartment listed on My Home/Your Home. The details of the place said it was on the same property with the owners. No address. A map showed the vicinity but not the address.

Usually you couldn't get an address to these vacation homes until you made a reservation. They had an opening for tomorrow night. I got out a credit card and booked it. I already had an account with them, so it was easy. A few minutes later, I had their address. It was almost too simple. I put the address into my phone and got directions.

"Colin Moore has relatives in Oro Valley," I said. "I've got the address. I want to see if he's there. I shouldn't be long."

Jules made a noise. "No way are we staying here," she said.

"Shouldn't one of us wait here for Dad?" I asked.

"We'll put a note on the door that his phone is in his office," Jules said. "And I'll tell him he better call us."

"Come on, Mom," Mattie said. "We can't wait around here. It's torture."

I agreed. We left notes for Jake, and then we headed out. We hardly said a word to each other. It was nearly an hour journey to Oro Valley even though we were in Tucson almost the whole way. Tucson must be the longest desert city in the world. Maybe even the longest city period. The Catalina Mountains loomed up to the north, in front of us for part of the way and then on our right for a while. In the gorgeous March day, the mountains stood out stark and mysterious.

"I hope he's not lost in the mountains," Mattie said. "We'd never find him."

"Did he say something about going into the mountains?" I asked. I glanced in the mirror to see Jules. She shrugged. I looked over at Mattie.

"No," Mattie said. "He didn't say anything to me about any-thing. Jules neither."

We continued in silence again. I had to figure out what I was going to do once I reached the house. If they were anything like Colin Moore and his family in Oregon, they would have guns. Would they shoot us? Would they push Colin out the door and be glad he was gone?

Detective Reese was right. I should not be doing this.

But I was going to do it anyway. If there was any chance he had come here to hurt Jake, I had to know.

"It's a few blocks away," Mattie said. "Behind this strip mall."

"Watch for the car," I said. "An old blue Honda hatchback."

"What year?" Mattie asked.

"I don't know," I said. "She just said old. Would it make a difference?"

"Probably not," Mattie said.

I got off the main road and was soon in a neighborhood. Many tall palo verde and old mesquites lined the roads. Saguaros grew in many front yards. I drove slowly. We saw few people out. Some dog ran out from one yard and started barking at us. I resisted the urge to flip it off. Or run it over.

"When we find Dad safe and sound," Jules said, "I'm gonna kill him."

"Me, too," Mattie said.

"Me, three," I murmured.

"This looks like a nice neighborhood," Mattie said.

"You sound surprised," I said.

"When I think of him," Mattie said, "I figured he grew up in a bad neighborhood or something. Why else would he turn out the way he did?"

We passed by a couple on the sidewalk. They waved. I nodded to them.

"He came from a middle class family," I said. "Maybe he had trouble with his parents. I don't know. It's more likely that he grew up feeling privileged, white male privilege. When things weren't turning out for him, he felt he had a right to pick up a gun and kill people. In many ways, it's cultural."

"That doesn't let him off the hook," Jules said. "I get frustrated, too, but I wouldn't do that."

"I'm not meaning to let him off the hook," I said. "He chose to do what he did. He was mad because some girl wouldn't date him."

"Misogynist little prick," Jules said.

"Yep," I agreed.

"That's the house," Mattie said. "506."

A small adobe-like house, similar to all the others in the neighborhood. No blue Honda in the driveway or on the street.

"If we see him, are we gonna kidnap him and make him take us to Dad?" Mattie asked.

I looked over at him. "No!"

"What are we going to do then?" Mattie asked.

"I haven't got that worked out yet," I said.

I drove down the block and turned the car so that it was out of view. Then I turned and looked at my kids. "Don't get out of this car," I said. They stared at me.

I got out and walked down the sidewalk. I glanced back. Both kids were watching me. I turned the corner. I felt like I was walking in slow motion. Or through water. I hadn't seen the creep since the trial. I didn't want to see him now.

I got to the house.

I walked up the sidewalk.

What was I doing?

This was crazy.

I walked up the steps. And I rang the doorbell.

A perfectly average normal-looking white guy opened the door. He smiled. I wanted to punch him. He felt so safe and secure in the world that he could open up his door to strangers?

"May I help you?" he asked.

"Is Colin Moore here?" I asked. Didn't think about it ahead of time. It just came out.

His smile faded.

Good.

"What?"

"He escaped from prison," I said. "You are a relative. Is he here?"

"Are you police?"

I hesitated. I couldn't say yes. That was against the law.

"No," I said.

"Colin is not here," the man said. "We don't have any contact with him. I heard he escaped, and I called my sister, but she hasn't heard from him either. Are you a reporter?"

"No, I'm married to the man who disarmed your nephew after he murdered someone we loved," I said. "And my husband's never been the same. Your stupid nephew ruined our family!" I suddenly realized I was screaming at this stranger.

"I told you: He isn't here."

"How do we know you're not lying?" I asked. "How do we know he isn't here, and he's planning on hurting more people?"

"Get off my porch," the man said, "before I have to get my gun."

"Your gun?" I said. "So you can be like Colin? It figures. If you see him, tell him the police are everywhere here. They will protect anyone he is after, and they're not afraid to use deadly force."

I heard the door slam as I turned and hurried down the sidewalk. I suddenly felt incredibly exposed. What if Colin was there and he had a gun pointed at me now. Or what if his uncle was getting his gun? I shouldn't run, right? That would make them more likely to come after me. No, no, that was a mountain lion, not a psycho man or a psycho man's psycho relatives.

I started to run, and I didn't stop until I got to the car. I got in, turned on the car, and drove quickly away.

"Was he there?" Jules asked.

I shook my head. "Who knows? His uncle was not happy I was there."

It seemed we were home again in minutes, and it never takes a few minutes to get anywhere in Tucson.

As we drove down our drive, we all leaned forward expectantly: We wanted to see Jake's truck. But we were disappointed. Instead another car—a black sedan—was parked where Jake's truck should be, and it looked like two plainclothes police were standing next to it. Police?

Oh no, oh no, oh no.

Chapter Thirteen

As soon as I stopped the car, I jumped out and called, "Did you find him? Is he OK?" Please, please, please don't let him be dead.

The woman came forward first and held out her hand. I had stopped shaking hands at the beginning of the pandemic. Wasn't gonna start now.

"Have you found him?" I asked, ignoring her hand.

"No," the woman said. "I'm Detective Brown and this is Detective Smith." Smith was a man. That's not their real names, but I don't want to remember their real names. I don't want to remember anything about them at all.

"Why are you here?" I asked. The kids came and stood next to me.

"Why haven't you found him?" Jules asked.

The woman glanced at the man police who was now standing next to her. "He's a grown man," she said. "People are allowed to go away. Doesn't mean they're missing."

Jules made a noise. "My dad would not leave without telling us."

"We hear that a lot," the man said.

"You hear that men just go out one morning and then disappear?" I asked.

"We do," the man said. "They get tired of their lives and they go away. Sometimes they come back, sometimes they don't."

Mattie groaned. Or something. It was almost guttural. I reached for his hand and held it.

"And those men who don't come back, do you look for them?" I asked. "Maybe they don't come back because something happened to them. Can't you trace his truck?"

"We put out a BOLO on the truck," the woman said. "No one has seen it. We can't trace it any other way because it's too old. We did look him up. We found out he was involved in a school shooting."

Something about the way she said it pissed me off.

"Involved in a school shooting?" I said, my voice rising. "For one thing, when I called in the report I mentioned that the kid who did the school shooting had escaped from custody and might be on the way down here. The only way Jake was involved in the shooting is when he stopped the boy from killing any more people!"

"Ma'am, you seem upset," the woman said.

That was the understatement of the day. I took a deep breath.

"Are you looking for my husband or not?" I asked. "If you are, what do you need from us, if you're not, we've got things to do."

"Since we're here," the man said, "we could look around. Maybe you missed something."

I glanced at the kids; they were stone-faced. "Like what?" I asked. "His truck? It isn't here!"

"We're trying to help," the woman said, "but there isn't much we can do unless we know he's in danger."

"The fact that he is missing should tell you he is in danger," I said. I had seen enough movies that I wasn't going to let them rummage around our property without a warrant. And I remembered too well what had happened after the shooting: they had searched our house to make certain—they said—that Jake had no ties with Colin, the killer boy. We never got the house back in order.

"Is there some reason you don't want us to look around?" the man asked.

"My dad isn't here," Mattie said. "That's the reason!"

The male shrugged and then said, "Maybe ICE took him."

"Why would ICE take him?" Jules asked. "He was fucking born here. His ancestors have been here a lot longer than yours or anyone in this asshole government who is snatching people from the streets like we're in Nazi Germany!"

The officers looked at me. Like I should reprimand Jules, stop her. No way. I looked at them. "Answer her question."

The woman said, "It was only a thought. If he's a citizen, he'll be all right."

"You mean if he's a citizen and hasn't criticized the federal government, right?" Jules said. "Because we now live in the United fascist state of America!"

"Here's a thought," I said. "Since you're the goddamn police who should be looking for this missing father and husband and citizen, why don't you contact the federal government to see if they kidnapped my husband and their father?"

It had not occurred to me that the government could have taken him. Why didn't it? Jake had been worried about this happening. He had worried about returning to Arizona because we were so close to the border. So many lies had been told about migrants—about everything. Whenever Jake mentioned that I didn't understand what it was like to be a brown-skinned man in this country, I would snap back that he didn't know what it was like to be a human woman on this planet.

We were both right.

Fuck. I hoped it wasn't ICE.

Just then, Tom drove up in his rental SUV.

"Who's this?" the woman asked.

None of your fucking business, I wanted to say.

"A friend," I said.

"Mom's boyfriend," Jules said. "You should talk to him. Maybe he did something to my dad so he could be with my mom."

"Jesus, Jules," I said. "Both of you go on in the house."

Mattie headed for the house. Jules hesitated, threw me a look, and then walked toward the house. The woman smiled slightly, as if to say, "Not fun when it's aimed at you, eh?"

Tom got out of the car and walked toward us. He had enough sense to keep his mouth shut.

"Unless you've got anything else for me," I told the police, "I'm going inside to try to figure out how to find my husband."

"Let us know if you hear from him," the woman said.

"Why?" I asked. "You aren't looking for him. What difference would it make?"

The man looked like he wanted to say something else, but he didn't. I didn't know why I was so angry with them: Maybe because they weren't doing anything to find Jake.

The police went back to their car, got in, and drove away.

"Obviously they didn't find Jake," Tom said.

"No," I said. "They aren't looking. Said he has a right to run off. He doesn't have a fucking right to run off. If he has done that, it will absolutely be the last straw." But if he hadn't run off, then he was in danger. Jesus. I was so tired of worrying about him. Be OK, be OK, be OK. "Tom, I've got to phone our lawyer. The police suggested Jake might have been picked up by ICE."

"Jesus."

"I know," I said. I pulled my phone out of my back pocket. "And my daughter suggested to them that you might have done something to hurt Jake."

"Man, she really doesn't like me," he said.

"She doesn't like anyone," I said.

"Aww," Tom said, "she takes after her mother."

"Shut up," I said.

I heard a Gila woodpecker alarming in a nearby palo verde. Could mean there was a hawk nearby. I glanced around, looking for the predator. I didn't like that birds of prey ate other birds. It seemed like bird cannibalism.

"Weren't you meeting friends?" I asked.

Tom shrugged. "They were boring. I thought maybe I could help here."

"How?"

"I dunno," he said. "I could look for Jake's truck. Check out some of the local bars for him. Things like that."

"Would you? Man, that would be great," I said. I took out my phone, looked for photos of Jake and of Jake's truck. I sent both to Tom's phone. "There's his truck. You can see the license plate number on the photo. And there's a photo of Jake since you haven't seen him in a few years."

"Any regular hangouts?" he asked.

"No," I said. "At least I hope not." I typed in the address of Jake's work and sent it to Tom. "Maybe somewhere near here or somewhere near there."

"I'll check with you later," he said. He started to lean toward me, as if to give me a kiss or a hug, but he checked himself.

"Habit," he said.

I didn't say anything. He walked to his rented SUV, got in, and drove away.

I went into the house. The kids were sitting in the living room on their phones.

"Nothing about Colin Moore in the news," Mattie said.

"Jules," I said, "why did you say that to the police? That Tom is my boyfriend."

"Because he is your boyfriend," Jules said, without looking up.

"He isn't," I said. "I've explained that before."

"I don't believe you," she said. "I don't think Dad did either."

I wanted to tell her to fuck off, but parents are not supposed to say those things to their children. So I didn't. But man, I was tired of her.

"You need anything to eat?" I asked.

"We're not children," Jules said. "You don't have to feed us every two minutes."

Mattie said. "I could eat."

Jules looked up and rolled her eyes. "OK. Come on. I'll make us something."

The kids got up and left the room, didn't even look back at me, didn't ask if I needed something to eat. Do all parents eventually feel like their kids are little parasites that grow up into big parasites? I think so.

I shook my head. Jesus.

I went into our bedroom and shut the door. I looked around the room. It felt so empty. I sat on the bed, picked up Jake's pillow, and smelled it. It smelled very faintly of him. I sighed. Where was he? How could he do this to us?

I put the pillow down. Then I made the bed. I sat on the bench at the end of the bed—the one Jake was always knocking into in the middle of the night when he got up in the dark to go to the bathroom. I should get rid of it. It was a fucking hazard. I ran my hand across the wood grain. It was so lovely. Perhaps I could use it to burn everything down. That was the only way it would ever get better.

I called our lawyer in Oregon again.

"Hey, Stephanie," I said when I got her. "Any word about Colin Moore? Jake is still gone."

"Oh, Christ," she said.

"And the police aren't looking for him," I said. "They think he left of his own accord. Looked at me like they would leave, too, if I were their spouse."

She sighed. "No news on Moore. They're saying he's gone to ground. Police speak for they have no idea."

"Fuck," I said. "I wish they would find him and shoot him. Put us all out of our misery."

Stephanie didn't say anything for a moment. "I know it's been tough on you and your family, but they will find him. He's not coming down to Arizona."

"Unless he is," I said. "Unless he is already here and has taken Jake."

"That's not what's happened," Stephanie said.

"You don't know," I said.

"Neither do you," she said.

"The police suggested ICE had taken Jake," I said.

"Fucking assholes," Stephanie said.

"It's possible," I said. "It's been happening all over the country."

"I know. I repeat: fucking assholes."

"Can you call around, contact anyone you might know, and see if they have Jake? I wouldn't even know where to start."

"That's what they count on," Stephanie said. "I will definitely make some calls. Go look for Jake. Forget about Colin Moore."

"I have something else I need to talk to you about," I said. "I saw Jake's boss when I was looking for Jake. He said he'd given Jake a deposit to take to the bank. Ten thousand dollars in cash. He said Jake never took it in. I found the deposit. It was in Jake's car. It wasn't ten thousand dollars. It was ten dollars! I think he was trying to set up Jake."

"Jesus," she said. "That doesn't sound good."

"I called him when I found the deposit. He hasn't called back."

"You don't need to be dealing with this now," Stephanie said. "Let me call his boss. Sometimes when people talk to lawyers all their nefarious plans go out the window. Do you know anything about him?"

"No," I said. "I've met him a few times. Jake doesn't say much. I think he's one of these wheeler dealer types. Thinks he's a bigger shot than he really is."

"Do you think he would hurt Jake?" she asked.

"I don't know," I said. "I mean, I have no idea. What do you mean?"

"Nothing," Stephanie said. "Nothing. It's that he could have embezzled the money and then blamed Jake."

"Are you saying his boss did something to Jake?" I said. "He killed him to cover up his embezzlement?"

"No!" Stephanie said. "Look. Give me his number. Do you still have the deposit?"

"Yes."

"Send me a photo of it," she said.

"I sent his boss the photo," I said. "I'll send you what I sent him."

"It'll be OK," she said. "I don't think he hurt Jake. It's a misunderstanding."

"OK. Let me know if you hear anything about Moore."

"Of course."

We ended the call. I sent her the photo of the deposit. Then I sent her Jake's boss's name and phone number. That was a relief. Stephanie would make sure that part of it wouldn't go any farther. I hoped.

Gawd I was tired.

Jake, Jake, Jake. Where are you?

He had been gone for over 24 hours.

Was he in a ditch somewhere or in a bar? I didn't know if I should be worried or pissed. It would be so much easier to be pissed.

I phoned my in-laws. Isabella answered.

"Hello, dear," she said. She didn't sound worried.

"Have you heard from Jake?" I asked.

"No," she said. "Are you still looking for him?"

"Yes!"

"I didn't realize," she said.

How could she not realize?

"Izzy, do you know where he is?"

"No! I thought he was home, safe with you. Why wouldn't he be?"

"Colin Moore has escaped from prison," I said. "He's got relatives here. I'm worried he's got Jake."

I couldn't believe I was saying that out loud. It couldn't be true.

"No! That crazy kid? How would he ever find Jake?"

"I dunno, but he was able to get a gun, bring it into the school and murder someone!"

She didn't say anything. "We will look around here," Izzy said. "Maybe he pulled off the road and fell asleep."

For more than a day? That seemed highly unlikely.

"Izzy, can the kids come stay with you until we find out what's happened to Jake?"

"Of course," Izzy said, "but wouldn't they feel better with their mother?"

I made a noise. Clearly Izzy had never had a teenaged daughter.

"I can't keep worrying if they're safe and look for Jake at the same time," I said.

And Jules was being such a pain in the ass.

"And what if Colin Moore knows where we live?"

"I don't see how that's possible," Izzy said. "But of course, the kids can come here. You want us to come get them?"

"No," I said. "Jules can drive down. But keep in touch."

"I'm sure Jake is fine," Izzy said. "He knows how to take care of himself."

Does he though?

"Thanks, Izzy."

I ended the call. I didn't understand why she wasn't more concerned. Was it possible I was overly worried?

I went to the kitchen where the kids were sitting at the counter eating scrambled eggs and toast. Mattie looked up at me and smiled grimly and then looked back at his phone.

"Still haven't caught Colin," he said.

"I want you two to go to Grandma Izzy's," I said, "and stay there until we find your dad."

"That's over an hour away," Jules said. "I don't want to be away from everyone."

"I'd like you to please do this without arguing," I said. "I can't worry about you and look for your dad. If I know you're safe, I'll feel better."

"And it's all about how you feel, eh, Mom?" Jules said.

The doorbell rang. Mattie jumped up. "Dad!" he yelled. Guess he forgot his dad would have a key.

I followed him to the door. He swung it open. Jake's boss Stuart stood on the other side.

"Can we talk?" Stuart said.

"It's OK," I said to Mattie. I stepped outside and closed the door behind me.

Stuart and I walked away from the house a bit.

"You got my message about the deposit?" I asked. "It wasn't ten thousand dollars!"

"I know," he said. "I am so embarrassed that I worried you. I guess I misunderstood Gabby." He didn't look embarrassed. He looked . . . caught. "Your lawyer called, and I explained to her that it was all a big mistake."

I raised my eyebrows.

"I wasn't accusing Jake of anything," he said.

"Well, that's good," I said, "because he didn't do anything."

My phone vibrated in my pocket. I took it out and looked at it. From Stephanie. "All good. You can give him the deposit if he asks for it."

"I can take that deposit off your hands," he said. I pulled it out of my pocket and handed it to him.

"I took a photo," I said, "as you know. My lawyer has it, too."

He nodded. He seemed pleased to have the deposit back.

"We will forget this ever happened," he said. "I hope. I am so sorry."

I couldn't tell what was going on with him. He started to walk away.

"Stuart," I said.

He stopped walking and turned to me.

"I hope you didn't have anything to do with Jake's disappearance."

"Of course not," he said. "Why would I want him gone?"

"I don't know," I said. "Why did you want to accuse him of stealing ten thousand dollars?"

"That's not what happened," he said. "It was an error on my

part. I've-I've been under some stress. Divorce. You know, tough times."

"Uh, OK."

"We good?"

"I think so."

I didn't know.

Then he was gone. I went into the house. The kids were packed and ready to go.

"Be careful on those roads," I said. "Do whatever Grandma and Grandpa tell you to do unless it's stupid."

Mattie laughed. Jules rolled her eyes.

"We want to stay here and help," Jules said.

"It will help if you're somewhere safe."

"You think he's dead, don't you?" Mattie said.

I gasped. "No! He's not dead. He's probably drunk somewhere. We'll find him."

Mattie leaned down to give me a kiss. I put my arms around him and held him tightly. Jules hurried out the door. Mattie soon followed.

"Love you both," I said.

"Love you, Mom," Mattie said.

Silence from Jules. Or maybe she grunted. I didn't know.

After they left, I went into Jake's office in the garage. I poked around a bit more, looking for any clue to where he was. I didn't find anything. I picked up the manuscript of the book he'd written, My Last Drink, and took it with me. I locked up his office and the garage. I went into the house and grabbed a bag, stuffed the manuscript in there, along with some extra clothes, and then went out to my car.

I wasn't going to wait around for the other shoe to drop. Since the shooting, my life had been a slow-motion nightmare.

It was time to wake up. Or die trying.

Chapter Fourteen

Tom and I texted each other and decided he would look north and west, and I would check out south and east. It was a long desert town. It was going to take a while. I drove down Speedway and then ducked down side streets. Came out at Tanque Verde. Drove too slowly. Cars kept coming up on me.

"Jake, Jake, Jake," I said. "Don't do this. Where are you?"

I thought of the four of us going outside to look for birds yesterday morning. Was that only yesterday? We were looking for indigo buntings or at least some kind of blue bird of happiness.

Or was it all fake? Were we just pretending it was like old times? Someone had tried to kill Jake. He had witnessed someone murdering his friend. Nothing was ever the same after that. And why not? People experienced trauma all the time. Women feel it in our bodies every fucking day as we try to live in this culture. We don't become drunks and then desert our families.

I pounded the steering wheel as I looked around the neighborhood for Jake's truck. Of course some people do become alcoholics and drug addicts as a response to trauma. Some people shut down. Some people turn violent. I knew all that. Yet it still pissed me off that Jake could not get his shit together. I didn't want to admit that. I didn't want to think it. But it was true: I wanted him to fucking get over it.

I wanted our life back. I wanted to remember what it was like for Jake and me to cuddle in bed in the mornings when the kids were still sleeping. I would rest my head on his chest, in that place made just for me between his shoulder and chest with his arm around me, my leg bent and gently nudging his testicles or up on his penis as it hardened. We giggled and stroked each other and talked about how the day would unfold. Sometimes we would fall back to sleep and the kids would wake us up by jumping on the bed. We hadn't done that in years. When we had sex now, it was to get it over with. Quick, never changing, an obligation. Pro forma, as it were. It wouldn't be a big deal, really, if we were close in other ways, but I felt like I was always waiting for the next bad thing to happen.

I felt guilty that I didn't feel more compassion for him. I wanted him to be well. To be normal. That was it. I wanted a normal life again. I expected it. That was what I signed up for.

That was before the world went to hell in a fucking non-biodegradable basket.

Mattie texted me when they reached their grandparents' house. I was relieved. They were safe. Nothing could or would happen to them while Izzy and Santiago were with them. At least, that was what I believed.

But more than that, I didn't want them around. Jules was making me so angry I wanted to hit her. Hit her. My own child. Someone should have warned me how awful teenagers could be. Especially teenage girls. To their mothers.

Everyone had been angry with me for leaving Jake—or for making him leave. It hadn't helped that Tom moved to Portland soon after. No matter how many times I told people it was a co-incidence, they never believed me. It was ridiculous: As if I had planned to leave the love of my life for an old high school sweetheart with whom I had nothing in common. I was a librarian and a writer, for chrissakes; I don't think Tom had ever read a book. Besides a sports book, maybe.

Ugh.

I drove around for hours. Then I went home and called the hospitals again. I checked the credit cards: He hadn't used any since he got gas the day before. Called the police. They still weren't doing anything, believed he left of his own accord. Searched the internet for any word on Colin Moore.

I was exhausted and sick to my stomach.

Tom called. "Nothing," he told me. "Anything there?"

"No, and I sent the kids away."

"I ordered a pizza," he said. "I'll pick it up and come over?"

"No," I said. "I'll meet you at your place. Get some beer, too."

The sun was going down. I hoped wherever Jake was he was not too warm, not too cold. Hoped he had water. Hoped he was alive.

We sat at the table in Tom's room and ate the pizza and drank cold beer. It was a relief to be out of the car, but that was about it. I told Tom how the day had gone.

"And my teenage daughter is acting out," I said. "She blames me for everything, including Jake's disappearance even though we don't know what happened. I'm so mad at him and so scared at the same time."

The room smelled of pizza and Old Spice. Or something like it. I looked around. Were all hotel rooms now so dingy? Paneled walls. Unoffensive art. In this case desert scenes. A bed. Table and chairs. TV.

"Jules still believes I left her father for you," I said.

Tom didn't say anything. He chewed on his pizza, swallowed, and then took a swig of beer.

"What?" I asked. "Nothing to say?"

He shrugged. "You asked me to come out then. Just like you asked me to come out this time."

"I didn't ask you to come out this time. You had business out here."

He grunted or laughed. I wasn't sure which. "What kind of business do I have out here? You said you needed me, so I came."

I shook my head. "No. I said it would be nice to see you."

He picked up his phone from the table and began scrolling. Then he stopped and handed it to me. I took it. On the screen were texts between us from a month or so ago. I read them and then handed the phone back to him.

"You said you had split up from Margaret again and needed a vacation. I suggested you come out here."

He read, "'Why don't you come here. I'd love to see you. I need a friend right now.'"

I rolled my eyes. "That doesn't mean I was begging for you to come out here."

"I never said beg," he said. "Why did you want me to come out?"

"I don't know anyone here," I said, "and you're easy to be around."

"Because I do whatever you want?" he asked.

"Give me a break," I said. "You've never done anything you didn't want to do."

"True."

"We've been friends for a long time," I said, "and we've had sex. So there's none of that sexual tension with us."

"Speak for yourself," he said.

I laughed. "We don't do that anymore," I said. "Besides it was never as much fun as it was when we were first together."

"What are you talking about?"

"You know," I said. "We learned how to have sex with each other. We knew each other's bodies. Once we broke up—"

"—and then came back together."

"Yes. You'd clearly had sex with other people, and it wasn't as good any more. You used your tongue in my mouth like a drill—your penis, too. And I remember you told me to be still. You didn't want me moving around."

"Yeah, I was a kid," he said. "What did you want? Besides, when you moved around, I was worried I would orgasm too quickly."

"You should have been worried if I was having fun or not," I said.

Tom looked embarrassed.

"It's OK," I said. "Twenty years later you were better again. No drill sergeant."

We both laughed.

"You never liked my tongue in your mouth," he said.

"Or anyone's," I said. "It's disgusting. Like a worm. Or a snake."

"Oh man," he said. "Why did you say that? Now I'll be thinking about that every time I have sex."

"Margaret liked your tongue, eh?"

"Are we really gonna do this?"

"No," I said, dropping my piece of pizza. "This pizza is horrible."

"Jesus," he said. "You don't like anything, do you?"

"Not tonight," I said. I sighed. "Why did you come out? Why are you here?"

"You know why," he said.

We stared at each other for a few seconds, and then he pushed his paper plate away and rubbed his eyes.

"I gotta tell you something," he said.

My stomach did a little dance. "What? You're leaving me for another woman?"

He smiled, although it was more of a grimace than a smile.

"I met with Jake yesterday," he said. "At Agua Caliente, before I met you."

"What?"

I suddenly felt fuzzy. Like I was going to black out or throw up.

"What do you mean you met with him?"

"He texted me. Said he knew I was coming to town and he wanted to talk with me."

"And you're telling me this now?"

"I was trying to figure out how to fit it into the conversation," he said. "There haven't been a lot of lulls."

"Jesus Christ," I said.

"It was nothing," Tom said. "He said he was glad I was visiting. Said you needed friends around right now."

"Why right now?" I asked.

"He said he was thinking of going back to teaching and that was making you nervous."

"OK," I said. "But why didn't he tell me? Why didn't you tell me?"

"Jake asked me not to," he said. He cleared his throat. "He also asked me to take care of you if anything happened to him."

Now I wanted to punch Tom.

"What the fuck, Tommy? You didn't think it was important to tell me that?"

"It didn't sound like anything," he said. "It's how guys talk to each other. So that we know we're OK with each other."

"Right. Has another man ever asked you to take care of his

wife if anything happened to him, the wife that you used to fuck?"

"I knew you would take this wrong," Tom said. "It was a throwaway request. I agreed, and we went on to other things."

"You agreed?" I said. "You didn't ask him why he was making this request?"

"No."

"Jesus," I said. "Sometimes men are so fucking annoying. Your lack of curiosity is astounding. Didn't you wonder if something was wrong with him or wonder if he was going to kill himself or otherwise desert his family?"

"No!" Tom said. "Nothing you have ever told me about him over the last twenty years would lead me to think he would do any of those things."

I felt newly panicked. Was he suicidal? Was he ill?

"What else did you talk about?"

Tom shrugged. "That was about it. He asked me how I thought the Tigers would do this season."

I almost laughed. "Like Jake gives a crap about the Tigers. Did he even know they are a baseball team?"

"I assumed so," he said.

"Essentially you were the last person to see Jake," I said.

"What? No. I'm sure other people saw him. I watched him leave."

"In his truck?" I asked. "So you didn't need a photo of him or his truck. That would have been a good time to tell me about your meeting."

"Yeah."

"Did something happen?" I asked. "Did you two get into a fight? Did you hurt him?"

"Are you really asking me these questions?" Tom said. "No, we didn't fight. Nothing happened. We had a conversation. We shook hands, and then he left."

"You shook hands?" I said. "God damn it. I've told him not to shake hands. That's how you catch stuff."

"I think that's the least of his problems now."

"Why would you say something like that?"

"I'm sorry, I'm sorry. I don't know what to say! You don't really think I had something to do with him disappearing?"

I looked at him. I had known him most of my life. I couldn't imagine him ever harming another person. But then I had seen too many true life murder shows on TV, and it felt like a lot of nice men were going around killing people. Mostly women, of course.

And then there was the time he beat me and left me in the woods. But we had been kids then. He had never done anything like that again. At least as far as I knew. Still, I couldn't see him hurting Jake.

"No, I don't think you did anything to Jake." I sighed. "I don't know what to do, Tommy. He doesn't have his phone, so he can't get a hold of me. If he's drunk and passed out somewhere, I'll never know. If he's hurt, I'll never know. Jake and I used to talk, Tommy. You and I never had anything to say to each other."

"Hey!"

"You know what I mean. Jake and I could talk for hours."

"That sounds exhausting," Tom said.

I laughed. "It wasn't. We talked about movies, books physics."

"Physics?"

"He studied quantum physics in college," I said, "but he decided to go into teaching instead."

"People have kids," Tom said. "Things change. You don't have time to talk about things like that."

"Is that what happened with you and Margaret?"

"I dunno. I thought we were living life like we always did.

You know, after I came home again. Everything seemed the same. Nothing changed."

"Maybe that's the problem," I said. "Nothing changed. You were still doing the shit that drove her crazy."

"I am who I am," he said. "I like what I like. I can't help it if she doesn't like what I like."

"But do you like her?" I asked.

"Sure," he said. "She's good people."

"She's good people?" I said. "Lord. What do you say about me?"

"You're not good people."

I picked up a pizza crust and threw it at him. Since he was only a foot away from me, I hit him.

"I don't talk to people about you," he said.

"Not even people we both knew?"

"No," he said. "What would I say? Um, remember when I moved to Oregon a few years ago? Well, I went there to be with my high school sweetheart, but in the end she dumped me for her husband."

"What did you tell your friends about moving to Oregon?"

"I had work, and then I didn't have work. You know guys. We don't ask a lot of questions."

"I never meant to hurt you," I said. "I actually didn't think you cared."

"I moved across the country," he said. "Of course I cared."

"You never told me how you were feeling one way or another," I said. "I can't read minds. Besides, you knew it would be Jake. You must have known. I told you that. He is the love of my life."

"I used to be the love of your life," he said.

"That's stuff we said to each other when we were kids," I said. "Besides, you never agreed with me when I said that."

"I told you I loved you," he said. "What more did you want?"

"Tommy," I said. "I don't want to do this now. Come on. You never really even liked me. You preferred hanging out with your friends and drinking and getting high. Or watching football. I bet you've never read a book. We had nothing in common."

"Lots of people have nothing in common," he said. "I don't even know what that means. I don't know what you mean when you say I've never read a book. There are lots of things that you've never done that I've done. So what? We had each other. We knew each other."

"You weren't Jake," I said.

"And apparently Jake wasn't me," he said. "Did you ever tell him you slept with me after you two started dating?"

I leaned back in my chair. "No. Why? Did you tell him? Is that why he disappeared? Did you tell him that?"

"You really think he'd disappear because I told him I'd had sex with his old girlfriend twenty-five years ago? Or however long ago it was. I'd have to tell him you cried the whole time and wished you were with him. I told you what we talked about. That was it."

I got up and went to the bed and curled up on it. "I want to sleep and wake up and it's all over."

"This is probably a bump in the road," Tom said. "Tomorrow it'll all be settled, Jake will be found, and it'll be all right."

I reached for my bag and pulled out Jake's manuscript.

"He wrote a book," I said. "My Last Drink."

"Is it his biography?" Tom came over and got on the bed next to me. He took the pages from me.

"I don't know," I said. "I knew absolutely nothing about its existence until today."

I closed my eyes. "I want to rest. Just for a minute. We can fight later."

A black screen came down over me. Then I heard Jake's voice in the darkness. He whispered, "Erin, find me." It was the first time I had heard my name in so long that I almost didn't recognize it. The name my Irish mother gave me, naming me after the land itself.

When I opened my eyes again, hours had gone by. It was dark out. Tom was propped up on a pillow next to me, holding Jake's manuscript in his hands.

"Any news?" I asked.

"Your phone has been quiet," he said. He handed me Jake's manuscript. "But I read a fucking book. This one. This ain't a man who is about to kill himself. Or disappear. It's all about his life with you and the kids. He loves you. He loves your kids."

"I know that," I said. "You don't need to tell me that."

"Maybe someone does," he said. "Because you're so fucking angry that you're barely looking for him."

"I've been looking for him for two days," I said.

"In bars," Tom said.

"Because I figure that's where he is," I said. "He's done this before."

"This isn't a man who is sinking," he said. "Read his book. Now, I've got to get some shut-eye."

Chapter Fifteen

Tom fell instantly asleep. I sat on the couch near a lamp and began to read Jake's story. He started out writing about his time growing up in Patagonia, AZ. It was a memoir, not a novel, although it read more like an outline of his life than like a real memoir. Most of it I knew. At first I wanted to read it quickly, to find some answer to what was happening, but then I started hearing his voice in my head. He was telling me his story. Of how he loved running along Sonoita Creek where he often encountered a large group of coatimundi.

He wrote, "They seemed oblivious to us as they nosed around in piles of leaves or in rotting logs. When I found out they lived in large groups of all female adults with their children, I was even more fascinated by them. Pedro hated that. He called them names and said they had chased all the males away. Pedro was kind of dumb about things like that. He never understood science. Or anything, really."

I smiled. That was true.

"And then in the open field, wild turkeys roamed. I could

hardly tell the males from the females until the males would stand up straight and fan out their tails. As a kid, I couldn't imagine anything more beautiful. That was before I saw an indigo bunting. My pops pointed a male out to me one day at the bird feeder he had just put up in the back yard, not far from the creek. It felt like I was seeing the sky in his blue feathers. Pops told me if I ever found a blue indigo bunting feather, I would be set for life and everyone I loved would be healthy and happy. I found indigo feathers, but they were never blue. Something happened to them once they fell off the bird, or maybe the blue was a trick of light. I never knew."

Then he wrote about getting older. He didn't run in the woods as much. He wrote about acting as a cover for his brother Pedro so he could date Josie. Wrote about drinking too much for a while. But then he stopped. Didn't sound like it took much effort.

He didn't have much to say about college until he met me. He thought I was fierce, a force of nature, beautiful, loving. He wrote about me like I was Wonder Woman or something. He was in awe of me.

I made a noise. In awe of me? I didn't get it.

He could talk to me about anything, he said.

Only he didn't. He didn't tell me about his drinking or about his brother and the baby.

I kept reading. Fortunately he didn't write about our sex life. He did say he knew immediately that he wanted to be with me the rest of his life.

I skimmed forward until we got to Oregon. Until the day of the shooting. He didn't go into detail.

He said, "Colin shot Horace Miller. Then he raised the gun and aimed at me. He called me a name. Somehow I grabbed the gun. The police came. Horace died. All I could think about was

Erin and the kids. I wanted them to be all right. I wanted them to know I wasn't dead.

"For a long time after, people treated me like I was dead. Everyone pulled away from me. My wife and kids had fear in their eyes every time they looked at me. I couldn't get used to that. And I kept hearing Horace's last breath. He struggled, and then there was nothing, and I couldn't do anything except take the gun away. I've dealt with men like this boy my whole life. They aren't connected to anything and they know it, so they destroy the world."

Tom began snoring. I tried to relax my shoulders, to breathe, as I kept reading.

Jake wrote very little about the aftermath, very little about us splitting up for that year, very little about drinking and driving with the kids. It was all about how much he loved us and our life. He was excited about returning home to Arizona. He wanted us to realize how beautiful life was in spite of the shooting, the pandemic, climate change, the destruction of our country.

"For a long time, I remembered the last drink I had: my last drink. The place, the time, how it tasted, because it felt like I was losing something by giving it up. Now I don't care about that last drink. Or any drink. It is fading from memory. I am now clear about what is important: Erin and the kids. I will do anything to make sure they are happy and safe.

"Despite everything, I still believe in magic. Not the kind of magic with wizards but the magic of an acorn, a seed, the magic of a bird flying across the sky—how do they do that? The magic of a bird leaving behind a feather that acts as a sign in our lives. Or as a gift, a gift that reminds us happiness is possible even when an easy life seems out of reach."

That was the last paragraph he wrote and the last sentence.

Tom was right. Jake was not trying to get out of his life. He wasn't suicidal. He wasn't fooling around. I knew that an addict could slip on a dime and drink or use again, but this didn't sound like a desperate man. I had been so angry about the loss of our life before that I couldn't see who Jake was now. He wasn't less than. Our life wasn't less than. It was different. He still loved me, still loved the kids. I was the one who had pulled away. He was the one trying. And now he was clearly in danger and had been for days, and I had missed it because I was angry with him.

Fuck.

I felt sick. I had to face the reality that something was really wrong. Something had happened to Jake.

It was early morning now. I had to find Jake.

"Tommy!" I thought I was whispering, but he started and sat up. He looked old and tired. Man. What a good friend.

"I read his book," I said. "You're right. He didn't leave. I've got to get my kids. We need to be together. We need to find him."

"You want me to come?"

I walked over to the bed and sat next to him.

"No!" I said. "I am so grateful you came out. I don't know what I would have done without you this last day or two. Feels like a month. But I've leaned on you too much since the shooting. I'm more comfortable with you than my own husband. I need to figure us out now. Go home." I kissed his cheek. "I love you, old friend."

I got up, grabbed my bag, and walked to the door.

"Let me know how it turns out," he said.

I nodded. And then I left.

I could hear my heart in my ears. It was still dark. The night was graying into dawn. I got in my car and drove away from Tom and eventually away from town as I headed toward Patagonia. Sunrise spread golden light across the hills as I wound down the road.

"Jake, Jake, Jake," I whispered. "Wherever you are, hang on. Hang on."

He wasn't drinking. He wasn't depressed. He had told me he was showing someone property, but he wasn't. It was a surprise. He was doing something to surprise me, to make my life better. What could that be? Obviously whatever it was, it went sideways.

The sun wasn't coming up fast enough. The roads were too windy. I couldn't get to Izzy's and Santiago's place fast enough.

By the time I got to Patagonia, the sun was nearly up. The sky was nearly blue. At their house, I jumped out of the car. I heard the birds all around, singing up the sun. The birds. That morning Jake had been all about the birds.

I didn't knock. I opened the door and called out, "Jules! Mattie! It's Mom."

Izzy called to me. "We're in the kitchen." They were all sitting at the round wooden table. The four of them looked at me with surprise. I was so glad to see them. Relieved. I felt like I had been asleep for the last two days—the last few years—and now I was awake. I looked at the table. How many years had I seen this table? The edges of it were green, the center was partly covered with dishes and cups.

"Mom, what's wrong?" Mattie asked. "Is it Dad?"

"You want some tea?" Izzy asked as she started to get up.

"No, no," I said putting my hand out to stop her. She remembered I didn't drink coffee. She knew that. Because she was family. Because she knew me. How could I have forgotten that?

"I'm trying to remember what happened that day," I said. "When your dad went missing. He didn't leave on purpose. I know that now."

"On purpose?" Jules said. "Of course he didn't."

"I mean I think he needs us to find him," I said. "Do you remember anything else he said in the car that day? Or in the morning when you were listening to the birds, during bird hour."

Mattie bit his lip. "We talked about birds. And he brought up the story about indigo bunting feathers bringing joy or happiness."

"He did mention to me that you didn't seem very happy," Izzy said.

"Me?" I felt a twinge of anger, and then I shrugged it off. Yes, he was right: I was not happy. I felt like my family was a pain in the ass.

"And he wanted to figure out a way to make you happy," Izzy said.

I laughed. I couldn't help it.

"No one can make another person happy," I said.

"Why not?" Jules asked. "A person can make us miserable so why not happy? Dad wanted to make you happy."

"He said he wanted to find a feather for you," Mattie said. "A blue one."

"We've been looking for one for years," I said. Why would he think he could find one now? It didn't matter. What if that is what he had been doing?

"When did he say that?" I asked.

"The morning he disappeared," Mattie said. "I didn't remember it, but I saved the Wizard bird recording from that morning, and I listened to it just now, and you know how it records everything, not only birds, and Dad said he wanted to find you a blue feather."

Oh my god. That was it.

"Where would he look for an indigo feather?" I asked.

"The Paton Center," Santiago said, "or our old house."

"We already checked The Paton Center," Jules said. "They hadn't seen Dad, and his truck wasn't there."

"Someone lives at your old house," I said. "They would have contacted you if Jake was there."

"You never listen to anything anyone says," Jules said. "They moved out a month ago. Grandpa has been digging holes and looking for treasure again. You told us not to go there so we wouldn't fall in the holes."

"Yes, yes, sorry. I forgot. Shit. Has anyone been there in the last couple of days?"

Santiago shook his head. "Not that I know about."

Izzy put her hand over her mouth. "He could have fallen into one of those holes."

Santiago shook his head. "No. They're not deep enough and I've filled most of them in. Well, except for a couple."

We all jumped up and headed for the door. Izzy and Santiago got into their truck. I got into my car with the kids.

"Hurry, Mom," Jules said. "Hurry."

Down their driveway, down their road, out onto State Route 82. Too fast. I had to remember the kids were in the car. Couldn't get stopped. Couldn't get in an accident. Left down the dirt road, deeper into the desert—or the brush. Wasn't sure if Patagonia was actually in the desert. We bounced from pothole to pothole.

"If he didn't have water, he could have died," Jules said.

"People can live without water for three days," Mattie said.

"Hasn't it been three days?" Jules asked.

Felt like it had been three years.

"No matter what," I said, "we are going to deal with this as a family. All of us. Together."

"What about Tom?" Jules said.

"What about him?" I said, jerking the car slightly to the left to avoid a pothole. "He's a friend."

"He's not part of our family," Jules said.

"No, he's not, but he is my friend."

"Can we get there?" Mattie said. "Who cares about the rest of this shit. Jules, quit being a brat."

I could see Izzy and Santiago's truck in the rearview mirror just barely, covered in the fog of the dust I was kicking up.

I turned down the dirt driveway.

We all looked around, hoping to see Jake's truck. The driveway curved toward the house, a white one-story building with tall old pecan trees growing all around it, shading most of the large property.

Jake's truck was parked at an angle near the car port.

I didn't know if I should be excited or terrified. I stopped the car, and we all got out. I grabbed my water.

"Spread out and watch for holes," I said.

I barely heard Izzy and Santiago arrive. "I'll check the house," one of them said.

"Dad!" I heard the kids call out. "Dad!"

I hurried to the back of the house near the berry bushes, where the feeders used to be.

"Jake!" I called. I hurried up the hill toward the trees, watching for holes, calling out for Jake.

I stopped and rubbed my face. "Please be OK."

Where was he? Had Colin caught up with him? Had a serial killer grabbed him? Had ICE kidnapped him? Had he collapsed from a heart attack?

What? What? What?

Sometimes I hated this world so much.

"Jake," I whispered "Where are you? Don't leave me again."

"I never left you, Erin."

It was Jake's voice loud and clear. Where? Or had I imagined it? I could barely hear the rest of the family calling him.

"Jake!" I shouted. "Jake, where are you?"

"Erin! Fell in this damn hole."

It was real. It was Jake!

I ran toward the sound of his voice and barely stopped, barely kept myself from falling into a deep dark black hole. I blinked. I couldn't see a thing.

"Is it really you?" I asked.

"Yes, I'm here."

Something shifted—a cloud or my eyes adjusted to the dark—and I could see my husband at the bottom of this pit.

"Are you OK?" I asked. I felt the adrenalin rushing through my body as relief cascaded through me—just like when I found out he was alive after the school shooting.

"I hurt my ankle or foot," he said, "when I fell, and I'm thirsty."

"Catch," I said as I dropped the water bottle into the hole.

"He's here!" I shouted. "Bring a ladder."

My heart was beating so loud and so fast. Jake smiled up at me. I could see the boy I fell in love with and the man I had stayed with for so many years. He was there. He was at the bottom of this fucking hole.

"You look like yourself," Jake said.

I sat on the ground and leaned over the hole so I could be closer to him.

"So do you," I said. "You wouldn't believe what the last couple of days have been like. I thought you had run off with another woman, was afraid you were drinking, worried you may have embezzled from your company, thought Colin was hunting you or ICE had kidnapped you. Something weird is going on with your boss. But it didn't occur to any of us that you had fallen into a hole."

Jake laughed. "Um, me falling into a hole seems more likely than some of those other scenarios."

"Are you sure you are OK?"

"I'm good," Jake said. "I'm so glad to see your beautiful face. Being here has given me time to think about a lot of things."

"Me, too."

"Dad!" Jules and Mattie were both screaming as they came running. They sprawled out on the ground and looked down at their father. Jules started to cry.

"I thought you were dead!" Jules said.

"Are you crying because I'm not?" Jake asked.

Santiago and Izzy leaned over the hole.

"I told you these damn holes were dangerous!" Izzy said.

"Digging for treasure, son?" Santiago asked.

"Funny stuff, Dad."

Santiago lowered the ladder into the hole. I tested its strength, and then I got on the ladder and went down.

"Careful," Jake said. "I've been here a while."

The hole smelled slightly of piss and shit. And Jake. I dropped onto his lap, and we put our arms around one another and began to cry.

"I'm so sorry," he whispered.

"I'm sorry," I said. "I know I've been distant since the shooting. I've been so afraid. I've been angry."

We looked at each other. I could feel his breath on my face.

"I didn't think I wanted a family anymore," I said.

"At least not this one," Jake said.

I nodded. "It has been so tough."

We embraced again.

"You aren't responsible for my happiness," I said. "So quit trying."

"And you aren't responsible for my safety," he said.

"But if something happens to you, I will be ruined. I saw that so clearly these last couple of days. So I want you safe."

"Shit happens," he said. "And speaking of joy and happiness."

He reached into his breast pocket and pulled out a blue feather.

"I was going back to the car after finding the feather when I fell," he said. "So here is the feather that will bring you joy and happiness."

"I dunno," I said. "I don't think it brought you joy and happiness."

"But it did," he said. "You're here." He held the feather out to me. I took it. "May you know joy," he said.

"Hey! Can you two come up out of your hole?" Jules shouted.

"Can you stand?" I asked Jake. "I can be your crutch."

Gradually as he leaned on me, we got him up. Hopping on one leg and using one rung of the ladder at a time, he made his way up out of the hole. I came up after him.

Everyone hugged Jake and each other. Everyone cried. Jules even embraced me.

"Dad, why on earth did you dig a hole that big?" Jake asked. "It was so deep I couldn't get out."

"I had a dream once that I would find treasure deep in the earth," Santiago said. "And today that dream came true."

Izzy smacked his arm. "You are filling in every one of these holes starting tomorrow."

"Ready to go home?" I asked.

"I am home," Jake said. "With all of you."

"Dad, that's really corny," Jules said. "Even for you."

"Wait until we tell you everything," Mattie said. "You won't believe all that's happened."

"I'll believe it," Jake said.

An indigo bunting flew by us, landed on a nearby tree and perched there, watching us.

"Maybe he wants his feather back," I said.

Jake shrugged. "Too late."

I put my arm around Jake's waist; he put his arm across my shoulders. We began limping toward the car. Jules and Mattie both talked, one over the other, telling their father what the last two days were like. I glanced at his parents, and they smiled, their faces etchings of relief.

Jake kissed my cheek and whispered, "Thanks for saving me."

I said, "Any time."

About the Author

Kim Antieau's books include *The Monster's Daughter, Whack-adoodle Times, The Jigsaw Woman,* and many others. She lives in the Desert Southwest of the United States

Bold, uncompromising, and guaranteed to enthrall, the new imprint from Green Snake Publishing features rich and compelling characters in pulse-pounding narratives that will keep you swiping left when you should be asleep. Immerse yourself in great storytelling and stay up all night with our addictive books. You might end up tired, but you won't be disappointed.